GARGOYLES
gone A.W.O.L

To a . . .

First Published in Great Britain in 2013 by Hodder Children's Books. The rights of Clémentine Beauvais and Sarah Horne to be identified as the Author and Illustrator respectively of the Work have been asserted by them in accordance with the Copyright, Designs and Patents Act 1988.

First published in the United States of America by Holiday House in 2015

HOLIDAY HOUSE is registered in the U.S. Patent and Trademark Office.
Printed and Bound in December 2014 at Maple Press, York, PA, USA.
www.holidayhouse.com
First American Edition
1 3 5 7 9 10 8 6 4 2

Library of Congress Cataloging-in-Publication Data

Beauvais, Clémentine.
Gargoyles gone AWOL / by Clémentine Beauvais ; illustrated by Sarah Horne.
pages cm. — (A Sesame Seade mystery ; #2)
"First published in Great Britain in 2013 by Hodder Children's Books."
Summary: Eleven-year-old self-proclaimed supersleuth Sophie "Sesame" Seade tracks down the culprit behind a series of gargoyle thefts in Cambridge, England.
ISBN 978-0-8234-3205-9 (hardcover)
[1. Stealing—Fiction. 2. Gargoyles—Fiction. 3. Family life—England—Cambridge—Fiction. 4. University of Cambridge—Fiction. 5. Cambridge (England)—Fiction. 6. England—Fiction. 7. Mystery and detective stories.] I. Horne, Sarah, 1979- illustrator. II. Title.
PZ7.B380587Gar 2015
[Fic]—dc23
2014022685

by
Clémentine Beauvais

illustrated by
Sarah Horne

Holiday House / New York

CAMBRIDGE
MAGDALENE COLLEGE
JESUS COLLEGE
NORTHAMPTON STREET
BRIDGE ST
ST JOHN'S COLLEGE
JESUS LANE
SIDNEY SUSSEX COLLEGE
MICHAEL HOUSE CAFE
PARADE
TRINITY COLLEGE
GONVILLE AND CAIUS COLLEGE
CHRIST'S COLLEGE
CLARE COLLEGE
KING'S
KING'S COLLEGE
CORPUS CHRISTI COLLEGE
ST ANDREW'S ST
KING'S BRIDGE
QUEEN'S COLLEGE
PEMBROKE COLLEGE
DOWNING COLLEGE
DARWIN COLLEGE
FITZWILLIAM MUSEUM
TO SCHOOL

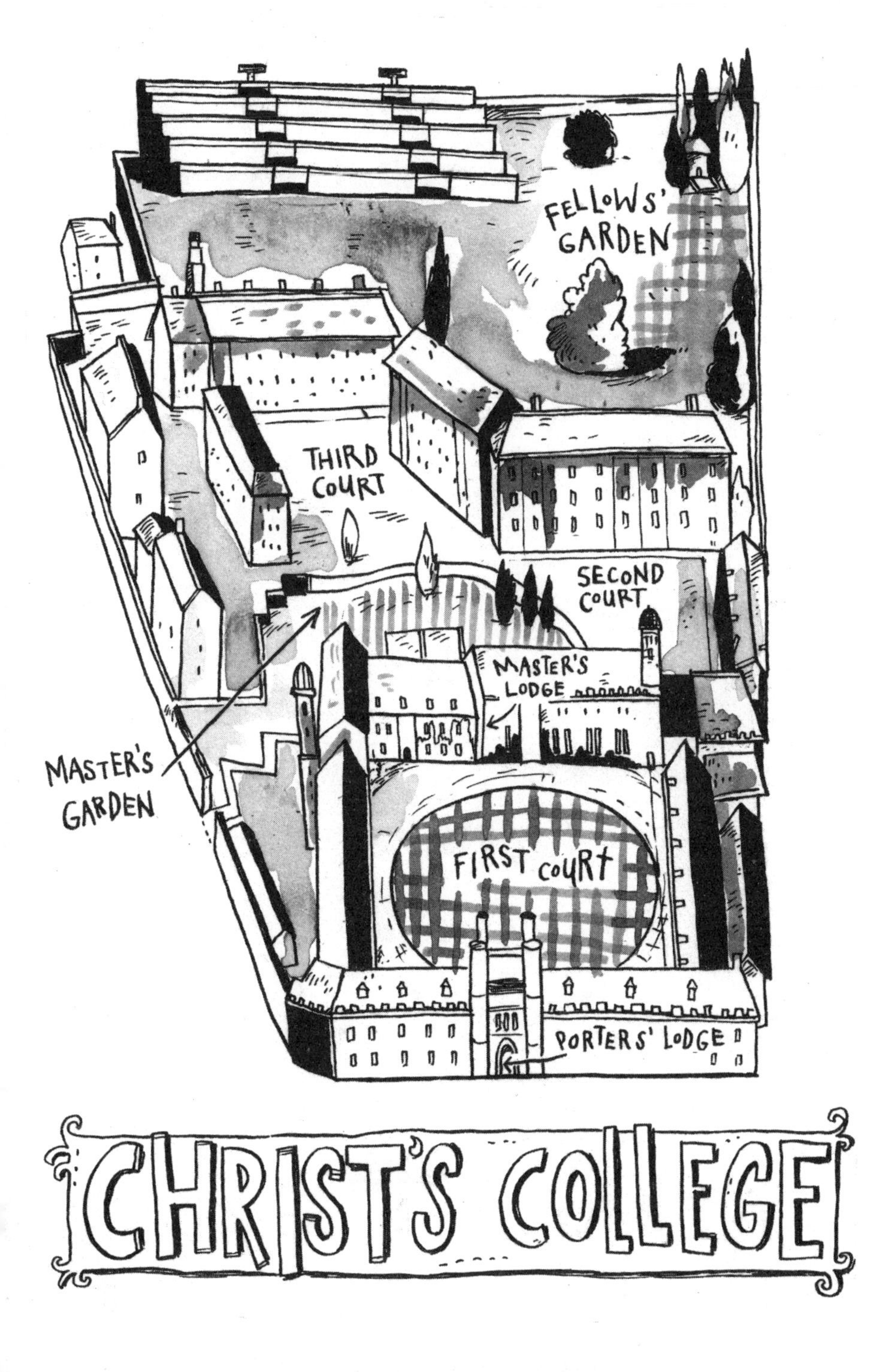
FELLOWS' GARDEN
THIRD COURT
SECOND COURT
MASTER'S LODGE
MASTER'S GARDEN
FIRST COURT
PORTERS' LODGE
CHRIST'S COLLEGE

I

It all began in a history lesson.

It all began with a buzz.

Buzz buzz!

Buzz buzz!

"*Who*," hiccupped Mr. Halitosis (Mr. Halitosis is our teacher), "*who*—*who* among you—*who*—against all the school rules—*who*—exposing himself or herself to the risk of being severely punished—*who* could possibly have brought a vibrating device—which, I can only conclude, is a *mobile phone*—to this classroom? *Who*? *Who*? *Who*?"

I must explain that "who" is not a good word for Mr. Halitosis to pronounce. Being endowed with the toxic breath of a nuclear power station,

Mr. Halitosis produces the deadliest *who*s on Earth. In this particular case, no less than nine of those powerful stink bombs were fired at us. By the time our eyes had stopped watering, it appeared that Mr. Halitosis had located the criminal, and planted himself in front of her.

And she was me.

"Sophie Seade!"

"Yes, Mr. Barnes?"

"You are buzzing."

"Do you mean buzzing with excitement at the thought of studying the Victorian era?"

"I do *not* mean that, and you know it. You have brought your mobile phone with you, and it has buzzed."

The other kids started sniggering a little bit, because my mobile phone is legendarily awful. While everyone else has a phone with a touch screen and a camera, my parents bought me one

that looks like I won it in a Christmas cracker.

"Give me your bag!" ordered Mr. Halitosis.

"No, Mr. Barnes, listen," I said. "It's not my phone. It's my pet hornet."

"Give me your bag."

"Honestly, it's Herbert the hornet. Sometimes he gets a bit bored and buzzes a lullaby or two."

"Sophie Seade, if you don't give me your bag . . . " said Mr. Halitosis. He reached down, which had the effect of squashing his beer belly like a space hopper ball, and he bounced up again, clutching my bag. "Right," he said, "where's that phone?"

"Nowhere. I'm telling you, it's Herbert."

"A likely story. Oh, surprise, surprise—look what I've found!"

And he fished out of my bag a red metal tin, shaped like a phone box, on which was written PHONE BOX.

In the manner of a coal miner who's found a diamond, he slowly twirled around with it so the whole class could see it properly and gape.

Gemma interrupted the general gaping. "If I were you, Mr. Barnes, I wouldn't open it. Herbert isn't the friendliest of Sesame's pets. I preferred Dinah the dormouse, but she got gobbled up by Peter Mortimer."

That brought a tear to my eye, because as much as I love my cat, I hadn't quite forgiven him for leaving Dinah's cleanly licked skull on my pillow a week earlier as if he thought I collected rodent skeletons.

Mr. Halitosis said, "Not very clever of you, Sophie, to carry your phone around in a tin marked PHONE BOX. It will be confiscated immediately and you can count yourself lucky I'm not sending you straight to the Head."

"It's Herbert that's going to go straight to *your* head if you open that box," warned Toby next to me.

But Mr. Halitosis didn't listen. Instead, he fiddled with the little lock, and suddenly the tin opened. I think he should have listened, because Herbert clearly wasn't chuffed to be woken up

by the poisonous stench of Mr. Halitosis's *"Oh! A hornet!"*

"Like I said," I said, and we all dived under our tables as if an earthquake had struck. Mr. Halitosis, unprepared, dropped the tin and rushed out of the classroom surprisingly fast for someone who doesn't eat any of his five a day.

Herbert, having run out of prey, swirled around the ceiling light for a while, then aimed for the window, crashed comically against the glass, and spent a good minute crashing into it again and again and again and increasingly angrily, before he found the next windowpane, which was open, and escaped into the sunny afternoon.

We emerged from our makeshift fallout shelters and Emerald crossed the classroom to open the door, revealing a Mr. Halitosis who looked just as furious as Herbert, though less stripy.

"That's it," he bellowed, "I've had enough! Sophie Seade, I am writing a note to your parents."

Everyone gasped with terror, for my parents have topped the Petrifying Parents list every year since school began. I have to admit I paled a little bit. Mr. Halitosis's ruthless pen had already started dancing the fandango on a piece of paper.

"*Dear Mr. and Mrs. Seade,*" he said out loud.

"It's *Reverend* and *Professor,*" I pointed out politely. "They don't go by *Mr.* and *Mrs.*"

"I couldn't care less if they're the Archbishop of Canterbury and the Empress of Mount Popocatépetl," thundered Mr. Halitosis. "*Dear Mr. and Mrs. Seade, I regret to inform you that your daughter Sophie is an ambulant menace to the peace and quiet of Goodall School. When*

she is not setting fire to her eraser or cutting her friend's bangs with nail scissors . . ."

"I'd asked her to do it!" pleaded Gemma.

". . . she thinks it is acceptable to smuggle phone boxes full of live wild beasts into the classroom."

"Wait a minute," I said, "that's not the clearest way of explaining it. . . ."

But Mr. Halitosis ranted on, *"I am sorry to say I believe it necessary for you to have a serious talk with Sophie*—and I have underlined "serious"—*in order to make her understand that being a gifted and intelligent young girl is no excuse for bringing chaos and desolation to the classroom. Yours sincerely, Joel Barnes."*

He crossly crossed the classroom and slammed the piece of paper on to my desk. "Get this note back to me tomorrow, signed by both your parents."

"Yes, Mr. Barnes."

"And if I have any reason to suspect that you have forged their signatures, I will call them myself."

I had to admit he'd won that battle. I was one hornet down, and a few hours from a very unpleasant conversation with Professor and Reverend Seade. Distraught, I slouched on to my desk and prepared for dark thoughts to invade my brain, but just then Gemma passed me a little note in red felt-tip that said:

So, why was your phone buzzing?

Only then did I remember that it had *actually* been my phone buzzing, not Herbert the hornet. I discreetly squeezed my ridiculous mobile out of my skirt pocket and clicked View Message.

And this message cheered me up to no end, because it was from Jeremy Hopkins, and it said:

Mystery disappearance at Gonville & Caius. Meet me there at three thirty. J.

II

As soon as the school bell rang, I switched to supersleuth mode and squeezed my feet into my purple roller skates. Jeremy Hopkins, Editor-in-Chief of *UniGossip*—the most sizzling-hot tabloid newspaper in the University of Cambridge—required the help of my extremely efficient brain. Have I mentioned that there are as many connections in my brain as there are stars in the universe?

"I don't know how many *times* you've told us that," declared Gemma on her scooter as we whooshed up the street to the city center.

"It's nothing special, you know. Everyone's got as many as that."

"But not everyone uses them to save the galaxy as regularly as I do," I pointed out. "By the by, what are you two doing, escorting me to town like this?"

"What do you think?" asked Toby, sitting up on his bike. "We're going to investigate with you!"

"What cheek! You can't just march into my mission like it's your birthright."

"If you don't let us," said Gemma, her pearl earrings shining in the sunlight, "I'll send an anonymous letter to your parents. I'm sure they'd be very interested to hear that you're the secret Chief Investigator of *UniGossip*."

"And what with Halitosis's note as well, they'll probably try to detach your head from your neck with an electric screwdriver," added Toby.

I have to admit I shuddered, even though my parents wouldn't have a clue how to use an electric screwdriver. Second battle lost today: I had to let them come with me.

"Is this another mission, then?" asked Gemma. "I thought you were already investigating something else."

"No, Jeremy shelved the case. There had been strange noises heard in Clare College Cellars, but we didn't find anything interesting. It was probably just a ghost or two having a night-time game of ghost rounders. What are you doing, Toby? You're cycling like you've entered a giant slalom contest."

"I'm practicing hands-free riding," he explained. "It's extremely cool: all the girls fall for it."

And sure enough, a thin, black-haired young woman on high heels who was just crossing the street found herself in the swerving path of extremely cool Toby, tried to avoid him, twisted her ankle on a cobble, and tumbled down to the pavement.

"Oh, well done," sighed Gemma, jumping off her scooter. She helped up the distressed victim of Toby's incapable cycling and asked, "Are you okay?"

"I have been better," said the girl with a slight foreign accent, glaring at Toby.

"Did you see your whole life flash by before your eyes?" I asked.

"No, just a couple of bike reflectors." She looked at me and frowned. "Have I seen you before?"

"It wouldn't be surprising," I said, "since this city is the size of my little finger. And not even as interesting." Which was true, as I'd just had a verruca removed from my pinky with liquid nitrogen.

"No," she murmured, staring into emptiness like a Greek oracle. And then the eureka moment came: "That's it! I remember. I saw a picture of you this very morning. With plaits, a little pink blouse, and no front teeth."

I started to tremble like a leaf that's seen a caterpillar. "Horror, how can that be? I thought there was only one copy of that shameful picture, and that it was safely stored on my parents' mantelpiece."

"Don't fret, it's still there," she said. "I had

tea at your parents' this morning. My name's Anthi Georgiades. I arrived at Christ's College a week and a half ago. I'm a visiting scholar from Athens. Your parents told me a lot about you . . . Sophie, is that right?"

"Not at all; don't believe a word they say. I'm Sesame. And these are Gemma and Toby."

We all shook hands—hers was unusually rough for someone who has tea with my parents—and Toby said, "I'm sorry for running you over. If I'd known you were pals with Sesame's mum and dad, I would have avoided you like the plague."

"Wish you had," declared Anthi. "Right, I'd better be going—what are you up to?

Something urgent, judging by the speed."

"Just going to Gonville & Caius College," said Toby, and before I could rugby-tackle him and stick a huge piece of black Sellotape on his mouth, he blurted out, "to investigate a mysterious disappearance."

"Toby!" hissed Gemma indignantly.

Looking a little intrigued, Anthi threw glances at the three of us and said, "A mysterious disappearance indeed? Well, that does sound interesting. I guess I'll catch up with you soon, Sesame. You can tell me more about it then." And she was gone.

"Quick," said Toby, "let's go, or Jeremy will think you've abandoned him."

Following his own order, he sped up the street like he was being chased by a troop of velociraptors. "I can't believe this," I sighed. "He went and told her that we were investigating a mysterious disappearance, knowing full well that she's in direct contact with my parents!"

"Definitely hide all sharp objects tonight," said Gemma.

A few more windy winding streets later, we ground our brakes to powder in front of the great gate of Gonville & Caius. The mission-crashers tied their vehicles to some railings, I struggled out of my roller skates, and we went up to see Jeremy Hopkins. Leaning against the wall, he was his usual disheveled self, sporting a holey *University of Cambridge* hoodie and Converse shoes from which the little toe of each foot was trying to escape.

"Good to see you, Sesame. You've brought your friends?"

"I had to: they're blackmailing me. Who's mysteriously disappeared?"

"You'll see. This way."

We walked into the first court of the college and were happily surprised to see that despite the warm April weather, it was covered with a layer of fluffy snow. "Oh, cool, there's a microclimate over Gonville & Caius," I exclaimed. "You should have told us to bring our sleds."

"Don't be silly, it's just the trees," said Jeremy, and he was absolutely right: the flakes were

dry and warm and loaded with little seeds. We stopped to watch the blossoms snow down from the trees onto the grass, and Gemma sneezed eleven times.

"Bless you, bless you, bless you, bless you, bless you, bless you, bless you, bless you, bless you, bless you, bless you," I said obligingly.

"When you've finished showering each other in snot and blessings, could you come this way?" asked Jeremy, who was holding open the door to the tiny spiral staircase which leads to his room. We followed him inside and wound our way up, only to find another surprise awaiting us.

"Wow, Jeremy! It's almost tidy in here!" I exclaimed. "I've never seen the color of your carpet before. Did you clean up on your own, or were you helped by the little animals of the forest in the manner of Snow White?"

"There's absolutely no reason to broadcast that sort of thing at the top of your voice through an open window," said Jeremy, and I realized that I was indeed standing next to the window and that half a dozen people downstairs in the courtyard were looking up at me like I was royalty on the balcony of Buckingham Palace. Jeremy murmured, "I just decided to go for a little change of lifestyle, that's all."

"It's lovely," I said, "it even smells of flowers in here, as opposed to smelling of foot fungus like normal."

"Ca't sbell adythig," interjected Gemma.

"I haven't brought you here to comment on the fragrances of my bedroom past and present," grumbled Jeremy. "Can we talk about the mysterious disappearance?"

"Sure." We all sat down on his bed. "Who is it

this time? Another student?"

"No. An object."

"What object? A silver chalice? A golden sundial? A completely unique nineteenth-century crystal sculpture of a tropical parrot with encrustations of ruby, jade, emerald and sapphire?"

"Not at all," said Jeremy.

"Couldn't have been," I said sadly, "because I broke *that* into trillions of pieces two years ago at that museum my parents took me to."

"Gemma," sighed Jeremy, "kindly put your hands over her mouth."

Gemma obeyed, but I would rather it had been Toby, because she then proceeded to sneeze into my hair since she didn't have any hands left to cover her nose.

"Right," said Jeremy. "This is what happened. Last night, at three o'clock in the morning, I was lying in bed thinking about the world and the meaning of life, when I suddenly heard a little noise outside the window—a tapping noise."

Just in case we didn't know what a tapping

noise was, he tapped my head three or four times with the tip of a lacrosse stick.

"So you looked out of the window to see what it was," said Toby.

Jeremy turned just a tiny bit more crimson than a strawberry smoothie. "Well, not exactly. To be honest with you, I couldn't be bothered to get up. So I stayed in bed and fell asleep."

"What a great detective you are," I snarled, but because of Gemma's hands over my mouth it just sounded like I was practicing growling in the manner of a mountain lion.

"And this morning," said Jeremy, "when I opened the window, this is what I found."

We all joined him next to the window, Gemma and I walking as if we were conjoined.

"What is it that you found?" asked Toby.

"Can't you see?"

We craned our necks and turned our heads 360° and leaned over the window-sill to our risk and peril, until Gemma finally spotted it. "Oh! One of the gargoyles is missing."

"That's right," said Jeremy. "The gargoyle just above my window has gone. Disappeared. Vanished. Evaporated."

And indeed there was no trace of the gargoyle, apart from the little pedestal onto which it had once been fixed. On each side of the missing monster stood its brothers, placed at regular intervals along the edge of the roof. They were ferocious-looking statues with open mouths which spat out rainwater when it rained. Not a rare

occurrence in Cambridge, rain. And one cannot be content with just normal gutters.

"Sorry," said Toby, "you called us here because a *gargoyle* is missing? When we could be at home watching TV and eating biscuits?"

"Wait a minute," objected Jeremy, "I never called *you*. Gemma, you can release Sesame."

She did, and I enjoyed breathing in air that hadn't been filtered through her sickly almond-moisturiser-scented fingers. "So a gargoyle's gone AWOL," I summed up. "Great. What do you want me to do?"

"Well, I don't know—investigate. Gargoyles don't spontaneously fly away. Someone must have stolen it."

"Yes, and you'd know who it was if you hadn't snored through most of it. Are you sure it's worth investigating? It's just a gargoyle. Why would *UniGossip* be interested in that?"

"Because, you genius, people don't steal

gargoyles for kicks. It has to be an international network of thieves, getting hold of old statues and selling them to multimillionaires to put in their houses in the Bahamas," Jeremy noted. "Listen, just do it, okay? I don't pay you to question my judgement of what is worth investigating and what isn't."

"That's right—you don't pay me at all," I said pointedly. "Whereas *I* spent a week's pocket money on that box of firecrackers I gave you for your birthday. Anyway, fine, I'll investigate."

"Good girl."

"We'd better start now, then."

The team immediately understood what the

next move was. It pleased me to have chosen such switched-on friends. Gemma and Toby gave me a leg-up on to the windowsill, and in no time at all I was standing on the edge of the slanted roof next to the missing gargoyle.

Through the open window I could hear Jeremy bawling, "Sesame! Sesame! Come back inside immediately!" Typical of adults to ask you to do things and then get all fidgety when you actually do them the most efficient way.

From up there the view was super nice: I warmly recommend it. You could see the snowing trees and the old mossy tiles and the

lacy stonework of the spires. But more importantly, you could see how easy it would have been for someone with a good sense of balance to take a stroll along the roofs with enough equipment to detach unsuspecting gargoyles from their pedestals. Not so easy, though, to carry them back down again—each of them was as long as my arm and definitely heavier.

Below me, Gemma and Toby popped their heads out of the window and Gemma asked, "What can you see, Sess? Any clues?"

"The pedestal isn't damaged at all," I replied, "so clearly the thief didn't have to break anything to get hold of the gargoyle. The statue must have been nailed to it. Maybe it was even just a matter of dislodging it."

I shuffled sideways to the next gargoyle to examine it. It stared at me menacingly, but I'm used to that with my parents. Anyway, it would have been scarier if it hadn't had a comical moss toupee on top of its head.

"That's weird," I said to Gemma and Toby.

"No, I was wrong, the pedestal's definitely part of the statue. They're made from the same block of stone."

I shuffled to the next one, which was even mossier, darker and grouchier than the last, and was faced with the same puzzling fact. If the thief had had to break the gargoyle from its pedestal, it would have made much more than a tapping noise. Even the deepest sleeper in Gonville & Caius would have peeked out of their window to see where the joyous clanging was coming from. And how could the pedestal look so smooth after that? Surely the thief wouldn't have spent two hours sandpapering it back to impeccable flatness.

Mulling over these mindboggling mysteries, I yielded to Jeremy's increasingly hysterical commands to come back inside, which had been the soundtrack to my little expedition.

"Finally!" he croaked as I leapt back into his room. "You and windows! I've never asked you to become the Cambridge Spiderman."

"How else am I supposed to investigate? I

know my brain's got as many connections as there are stars in the universe, but that doesn't mean I can solve mysteries by sipping tea in a tartan bathrobe."

"Please do try," said Jeremy. "Okay, what are your conclusions?"

"I don't have any," I had to confess. "It's extraordinarily mysterious. The pedestal isn't broken, when it should be, because the gargoyles and the pedestals are made from the same block of stone. It's weird. It's exactly like . . . "

And then I stopped, because I'm not a ninny, and I know *that*'s not possible.

"Exactly like what?" asked Jeremy.

"It's exactly like," said Toby, "the gargoyle just leapt off its pedestal into the starry sky of its own accord. Is that what you mean, Sesame?"

"Yes," I whispered, "but obviously, it can't have."

"Obviously," said Toby.

There was a significant silence, which Gemma rudely broke by sneezing again. "I have to get out of this place," she declared, wheezing

like a sickly shih tzu. "Anyway, it's time for Sesame to go home and get guillotined by her parents."

"Oh, excellent," declared Jeremy. "Enjoy." So we bid him adieu and walked down the swirly staircase to the whited-out courtyard. Gemma ran across the lawn to the great gate to get out as soon as possible, which provided the entertaining vision of a sprint runner in school uniform struck with episodic fits of sneezing.

I was following her at a more leisurely pace, when I realized Toby wasn't at my side like a good sidekick should be. Turning around, I noticed him standing near the staircase, and looking at the ground as if a trapdoor to Ali Baba's magic cave had opened up before his very eyes.

"What's up?" I asked, walking over to him.

He didn't reply, but pointed. And although I, Sesame Seade, am seldom spooked, I have to say I shivered just a tiny bit.

For the thin layer of white down from the trees was unmistakably scattered with paw prints.

In silence, we followed their neat little trail, and their neat little trail took us to a flowerbed not covered in tree snow. And in the earth of that flowerbed was one last clearly-molded paw print.

One that looked nothing like a cat's, or a dog's, or a rabbit's, or a squirrel's, or anything I'd ever seen roaming around our little city.

But then, Toby's the animal expert, not me.

"What is it?" I asked.

The animal expert shook his head and, looking up at the gargoyles with their disheveled manes and thirsty stone tongues, he whispered, "I have absolutely no idea."

III

"No need to tiptoe into the room in that grotesque fashion, Sophie, I can see you in the mirror."

My parents have a habit of putting mirrors in strategic places to keep an eye on me at all times. Sometimes I wonder if they've also hidden a CCTV camera in my bedroom, and a

microchip in my brain that reads my thoughts and types them out for them to read in their morning paper.

"Oh, hello, marvelous mummy of mine. I was just being very quiet in case you were asleep."

"I am generally awake at five in the afternoon, and in any case I don't tend to fall asleep while standing in front of the bookshelf. Where have you been?"

"Oh, y'know, just hanging out with the gang. Is my favorite father around?"

"The only one I can think of is at Evensong, as is, I believe, habitual for a vicar at this time of the day on Tuesdays. You can be forgiven for not having noticed this, since it has only been the case for the past eleven and a half years of your life."

And she resumed perusing the bookshelf, which, in case you're wondering, is not particularly well-stocked with fun children's books and colorful comics. The volumes fall into two categories: Mum's books about science,

and Dad's books about God. The only things they have in common are thickness and yawn-inducing incomprehensibility. Mum finally found the book she was looking for, opened it at the end, looked up something in the middle, closed the book, put it back on the shelf, and stared thoughtfully at the ceiling. That is what a lot of people in this city seem to be doing day in, day out.

She then uttered number four in her list of favorite questions: "Don't you have homework to do?"

"I'll get to that. But first allow me to express my concern for your well-being. You sound perturbed. What are the worries that are making those wrinkles on your fatigued face even deeper than usual?"

She rolled her eyes. "You are such a darling. None of your business. Though, believe me, you are responsible for many of these wrinkles. Go and do your homework."

"In a minute. I was wondering if you'd like to play a little game first, just to chillax."

"I don't have any time to play, and I don't want you to use such vulgar words."

"No, wait—listen—it's a super fun game. I blindfold you, I give you a pen, and we see if you can sign your name properly without looking at the paper. Hilarity guaranteed!"

Mum shot me one of those knowing stares that she's internationally famous for, sat down, and breathed in and out deeply. "Right. What is it that you need me to sign but don't want me to see?"

"What? I can't believe this. It's just an innocent suggestion! I'm always suspected of foul play in this house."

"For very good reasons. Give me that paper."

"Only if you promise not to shove me head first into the shredder."

"Certainly not; you would break it. Give me that paper."

I fished Halitosis's loathsome letter from my bag and did a slow walk of shame towards Mum, palms sweating gallons of water on to the paper, which sadly didn't even begin to

melt the ink on it. Mum snatched the note from me, and I watched her eyeballs jerk from right to left and from top to bottom until the whole message had been processed by her fearsome brain. Then she looked up at me, grabbed a pen from the table, and signed it.

"There," she said. "Now do your homework."

I gaped. And then said, "Dad needs to sign it as well."

"Leave it here, then. He'll sign it when he's back from Chapel. Off you go!"

I walked upstairs in a trance-like state. Even Peter Mortimer shooting out of the parental bedroom to drop a half-eaten white mouse on my foot didn't shake me out of my perplexity. Why hadn't Mum frogmarched me to the nearest cliff and pushed me into the abyss? Why hadn't she cut open my skull with an oyster knife and scooped out my brain on to a teatray? Why hadn't she sliced me into a carpaccio and served it to the guests in Formal Hall tonight? It was even more enigmatic than a Gonville gargoyle gone AWOL. I was so

surprised I inadvertently did all my homework.

"Can you believe it?" I asked Peter Mortimer who was lying down next to me on my bed. "What can possibly be on Mum's mind that she doesn't even tell me off for 'smuggling phone boxes of live wild beasts into the classroom'? That's not normal."

The animal yawned and stretched, not very interested. Only then did I realize that I'd been sitting on his tail for the past hour and a half. "What the deuce, Peter Mortimer!" I exclaimed, jumping to my feet. "You generally claw me to shreds if I so much as touch your tail."

But Peter Mortimer had fallen asleep again, his newly recovered tail coiled around him, as if nothing had happened.

"Not normal," I repeated pensively.

☆☆☆

When I walked into the dining room, Reverend Seade was in a state of profound annoyance—you can tell, because he turns turnip-purplish everywhere except for the rims of his nostrils,

which remain a beautiful creamy white. Thinking that divine punishment had finally caught up with me, I dropped my head and waited for the tornado of torment to hit.

But it didn't. Instead, Dad said, "Good evening, Sophie."

As it turned out, he was simply upset because he'd tripped over a loose stone outside Chapel and landed on his knee, which was now adorned with a bruise the color of fresh vomit. As for Halitosis's note, it was on the table, duly signed by both parents, neither of whom blinked when I pocketed it before sitting down for dinner.

They even said "Bon appétit" to me.

As if I deserved my onion soup.

It was too much.

"That's enough," I said. "Tell me off. Now."

"What?" said Mum in a tired voice.

"Tell me off for bringing chaos and desolation to the classroom!"

"Oh that," said Dad, sounding like a zombie who can't be bothered to hunt for brains. "Yes, that's not very good of you, Sophie. Don't do it again, please."

And they slowly slurped their soups, making the noise of a couple of half-hearted hoovers.

"Is that all?" I asked.

Neither of them replied.

"Am I still alive?" I asked again.

No reply.

"Do I exist? Can you hear me? Hello? Have I been killed and turned into a ghost?"

"Thank goodness not," snarled Mum, "you'd make this place the worst haunted house in the country. We are simply tired, my dear, by *work*. I know it is a concern you are not familiar with. Oh yes, and we meant to tell you—your father and I are going out tonight."

"What? Tonight? When tonight? It's already tonight."

"After dinner."

"Where are you going?"

They both sighed. "The problem with Sophie is that she's a nosy little Actaeon," said Dad.

"Well, if you're tired, shouldn't you be staying in bed with a nice mug of jasmine tea and a book of crosswords?"

"Thank you ever so much for the advice, Doctor Seade," said Mum, "but we've got better things to be doing with our time. You'll be okay by yourself?"

"Can I invite a few students around for a rave?"

"No, but you can do the washing-up."

And after dinner, just like that, they left! The cheek of it! Not telling me off for being a walking disaster—not worrying about me burning down the house—nothing. Irresponsible parenting at its finest. Vaguely worried that I'd lost my legendary talent at terrorizing the old and wrinkled, I waited until they left the house,

then skipped across the First Court of college and leapt into the Porters' Lodge in the manner of the pouncing grizzly bear.

"Sesame!" exclaimed Don the Porter. "Can't you make an entrance friendlier to the weak-hearted? You scared me!"

"Excellent, that was the idea," I replied, leaning against the high counter. "Listen to this: I'm freer than a fat-free freebie frisbee.

My parents have abandoned me for at least an evening. What do you think I should do with my time? I can't waste it watching TV. We don't have a TV."

"Well," Don said, handing me a box, "you could begin by opening this package. It arrived for you this morning, but your parents forgot to pick up their post today."

And sure enough, it was a package with my name on it, in a handwriting I'd recognize among all handwritings, for no one else's handwriting looks like they violently squashed a squad of daddy long legs on paper to form the letters.

"Triple hurrah!" I exulted. "It's from my cool godfather Liam!"

"The one with the dreadlocks?"

"Yes, that one!"

"The one with the nose ring and panther tattoo?"

"The very one!"

"The one your dad says they would never had chosen to be your godfather if they'd known he'd

turn out to be a good-for-nothing artist eleven years later?"

"Absolutely and indisputably that one," I confirmed. I then realized my fingers had been opening the package while I'd been chatting away, which was smart of them, and I looked inside. "Woohoo! He always has the most mega ideas. Last birthday the ravenous carnivorous cactus, last Christmas the freakish fireballs, and now this!"

"Goodness, what is it?" asked Don, recoiling into his swirly chair.

"A detective kit for aspiring supersleuths! With everything you need to capture criminals."

Don breathed a very long sigh of relief as I squeezed Liam's letter out of the package:

Dearest daredevil,

I heard of your spectacular jump for justice. Keep up the world-saving! Here's a bit of help for your next mission. No need to tell the parents, of course.

Godfatherly yours,

L x

"Zip up your lips, Professor and Reverend Seade aren't to know about this," I whispered to Don. "They think I'm retired from sleuthing. I'll run and hide it in my swim bag."

Having made Don swear he wouldn't tell, I skipped across First Court again and realized I'd put my key inside my left jacket pocket, which is the wrong pocket: it has a hole in it, due to having once hosted a hoglet for a whole afternoon. A hoglet is a baby hedgehog. The key had consequently fallen into the lining of my jacket. I started to scramble for it by putting

my whole forearm in the hole in the manner of the fisherman gutting a skate, and found many interesting objects I'd forgotten I'd lost. These included a yo-yo, a crème-brûlée-flavored stick of chewing-gum, a pound, Gemma's butterfly hairclip (that's where it was! She'd almost decapitated me for misplacing it), and, just as I finally reached the key . . .

"That doesn't look like the most convenient way of taking off your jacket, Sesame."

I turned on my heel.

(Actually, does one ever turn on one's heel? I think not: one would fall comically backwards like a bowling pin.)

I turned on the balls of my feet, and found myself face-to-face with lithe Anthi Georgiades, who'd swapped her high heels for black ballerina shoes and was now hardly taller than me.

"Oh, good evening!" I chimed. "I didn't hear you coming. I wasn't taking off my jacket, just looking for my key. Have you recovered from your close brush with death?"

"Well, I'm sure I'll have many nightmares of

chubby little boys on bikes, but that's all right. In fact, Sesame, I was just coming to see your parents."

"Tough luck, they're out. You can leave a message after the tone." We both waited for the tone. "*Beep*!" I said.

"Hello, Professor and Reverend Seade," said Anthi. "I was just calling to give you the soothing essential oil I was telling you about this morning. Here it is. Goodbye!"

"To re-record your message, key *hash*," I declared. She didn't seem to want to re-record. "Right," I said. "What's that about?"

Anthi handed me a small green bottle. "Well, your parents told me you're . . . er . . . an energetic child . . . a little bit turbulent, let's say—and I mentioned that I sometimes use essential oil to calm down and focus. I offered to bring some round to see if it would work on you. You just have to leave it open in your bedroom and it will spread into the air."

"Wonderful," I said, plowing as furrowed a brow as I could. "An international conspiracy to

pollute my airspace with toxic molecules of good behavior."

"You don't have to try it if you don't want to," laughed Anthi. "Okay, I'd better go—see you soon, Sesame."

It was getting dark outside, and the wisteria on the wall was all sweaty, like before a storm. I walked into the house, hopped upstairs to my bedroom and opened the detective kit under the dull gaze of Peter Mortimer, who hadn't moved one whisker since before dinner.

And a wow-inducing detective kit it was. No lame magnifying glass in there, I can tell you: this was high-tech sleuthing. There was a tiny videocamera hidden in what looked like a bit of stone, a mini-microscope, a fingerprint-detecting kit, an eye-scorchingly bright torch masquerading as a ballpoint pen, some intruder detectors and a skeleton key. That's a key that can open lots of different doors, not a key to the underworld of the dead and buried.

"Look at that, Morty," I murmured to the comatose cat. "I could take your

fingerprints if you had fingers."

But he didn't, so I took mine and observed them under the microscope, which then printed them on to a little square of paper. Unsurprisingly, since they were mine, they looked exquisite. I then followed the instructions to take fingerprints left on an object, using the bottle of *Soothing Luscious Euca-licious Eucalyptus Essential Oil* that Anthi had just given me. You first had to smother the glass in some fine powder, then brush it away with a tiny brush, and then you lifted it all off with a piece of tape. Once again, the microscope spat out a small square of paper with a perfect drawing of Anthi's fingerprints. As fingerprints go, they weren't too bad either. Little labyrinths at the tip of your hands. I wondered if bacteria got lost there sometimes.

And brutally the storm broke out. The room turned white with lightning, and a huge gust of wind slammed

the window shut, which was courteous of it since it meant I didn't have to get up from my bed. Less courteously, though, it also dislodged my geography notebook from my shelf, and it fell directly on the bottle of essential oil on my desk, shattering it to crumbs of glass and spreading toxic molecules of good behavior absolutely everywhere. Not to mention that it also threatened to drown my precious sheet of geography homework.

"Curses! Now I'm going to turn into a goody-goody like Gemma," I exclaimed.

I quickly squeezed my earlobes to check they hadn't yet sprouted pearls in the manner of wild oysters. Thankfully, they hadn't. But I had to get out of there quickly. Scooping up Peter Mortimer with one hand and my geography homework with the other, I ran out of the room, closed the door behind me and rushed downstairs.

Downstairs was as gloomy as my parents' taste in bedspreads. The sky outside was grumbling like a stomach, and the rain and wind were giving a good thrashing to the

wisteria. Peter Mortimer, who's usually even more scared of storms than of the vacuum cleaner, wasn't even vaguely fidgety. I put him down on the table, he stretched a little bit, and curled up.

"Where has this whole zen attitude suddenly come from?" I asked the animal. "Have you been doing yoga when I wasn't watching? Hello? Supersleuth to supersloth, do you copy? Is there still a brain between those two isosceles triangles?"

KRRK! went the thunder, but the supersloth didn't budge, even though I was now holding his head up by the ears like a soggy flannel.

"That's enough, Morty," I murmured. "You can stop being all nice and quiet now. I'm OK with the usual uncontrollable, horrible, detestable you. Come on, show me how much of an annoyance you can be."

But the monster just yawned. A flash of lightning later, and all the lights in the living-room went out with a sad little click.

"Oh, great. A power outage. Just what we

needed, Morty, isn't it? Well, good excuse to get the candles out."

In the darkness I could make out Peter Mortimer's eyes like two little car lights. They were going left-to-right, right-to-left, left-to-right, right-to-left, in the direction of the floor, to the rhythm of a bizarre little noise which half of my brain had clocked while the other part was thinking about the candles.

A funny little pitpatty sort of noise, a bit ruffly, a bit squeaky, a bit shuffly. And then lightning struck again.

And in the two seconds it illuminated the room, I saw it.

A *wave*.

No, a *tide*.

No, a *tsunami*.

A tsunami of bright white, furry, screechy, tubby, speedy *mice*. Flooding in through the half-opened sash window into the living room.

The good thing about being a supersleuth is that you are always as chilled as a satsuma sorbet. Even when perched on an eighteenth-century armchair when your living room is being recarpeted with mice (much nicer, in passing, than the old boring brownish carpeting).

"Peter Mortimer," I said, "pray, jump off that table and catch these mice."

The cat's shiny eyes closed in a way which indicated he was yawning. I changed tack. "Now look here, you extremely useless animal, you'll be the laughing stock of all the strays in the 'hood if you let these things invade the house. They'll stop sharing the best squirrel-slaughtering strategies with you. You won't get invited to any of the garden parties and all the eligible young female cats will know you as Loser Mortimer, the One Who Let In All The Mice."

Loser Mortimer, as far as I could tell, had fallen asleep. Once again, it was my burden and responsibility to save the situation.

My eyes had started to get used to the darkness, which was very helpful of them, so I planned my escape. In one jump, I landed on the extremely expensive mahogany dinner table. From the table I grabbed on to the exquisite Murano-glass chandelier and Tarzaned my way through space and onto the sofa, even though it's normally a complete no-foot zone. I then took the deep breath of the long-distance jumper, and leaped to the mantelpiece (shattering to pieces—alas!—the picture of my younger self in plaits and pink). Finally, I managed a formidable jump to the windowsill, from which a few mice were still rushing in, laundered by the rain to squeaky cleanness.

Stretching my right arm so much that it probably grew a few inches longer than my left, I reached for the door, pulled it open, and leaped out of the house and into First Court. The sky above was ripped by lightning.

"You are a disgrace to your race," I informed Peter Mortimer as I left. "I'm going to need to call the Porters to do your job. And if they're better than you, you can say goodbye to your pension scheme, your salary, your health insurance and your weekly bonus of tinned tuna."

Having expressed these well-deserved threats, I launched into the dark and stormy night, and reached the Porters' Lodge dripping like a sponge.

"You again?" exclaimed Don. "Why are you not in bed?"

"Because my bedroom is polluted with poisonous Euca-licious."

"Whatever that means, I'm sure your parents wouldn't accept it as a good excuse," said Don, picking up his newspaper. "Well, I guess when the cat's away, the mice will play."

"Precisely," I said. "And they've chosen our living room as a playground, which is a little bit inconvenient. If you had about three hundred mousetraps to lend me right now, with at least six wheels of brie to serve as bait, it would

make my life easier. Or stilton. Do they prefer stilton? My favorite cheese is roquefort. Maybe they'd be keener on that. I just don't know."

"Has anyone ever told you you should be a writer? You make up some entertaining stories," mumbled Don.

"No, listen—I'm not even being slightly funny. You need to come *illico presto* and help me meow the little things away from our living room, or else my parents will go and think I'm the one who invited them along. Seriously, darling Donald, shining example of porterhood, you have to believe me, it's Rodentland at Seade Towers right now and I'm pretty sure Professor and Reverend S. aren't the kind of people who like to sit on nibbled furniture."

Don glanced at me above his rectangular glasses like I'm in the habit of telling fibs, which is a vile rumor spread around by my parents. But he finally put his newspaper down, got up, and picked up an umbrella which turned inside-out in the wind and dislocated like a sad vulture as soon as we stepped out

of the Porters' Lodge. Don frowned, took a few steps back to build up speed, and crossed First Court in just five long leaps like an astronaut on the Moon during monsoon season. It would have been perfect had he not tripped on the uneven stone outside Chapel which had caught Dad earlier too. Can't adults watch where they walk? A vomit-colored bruise was sure to adorn his knee too.

I was about to follow him when I spotted a spot. Two spots, even. Three. Four. Five. On the dryish stone from the entrance of college to the stormy Court, where they disappeared, washed off by the rain.

A line of muddy paw prints.

And though it was raining cats and dogs, these paw prints definitely didn't belong to either species.

IV

"And this explains, Mr. Barnes, why my geography homework is currently in shreds and therefore un-hand-in-able. The mice went for it like it was a picture of a cat."

"I would not believe a word of all this, Sophie Seade, if I had not received a phone call from your father this morning informing me that it was

indeed the case. You will do your homework again for tomorrow, rain or shine, whether mice, termites or Tasmanian tigers have invaded your house."

"But Mr. Barnes, that's unfair, I've already done it!"

"Then it will be all the easier for you to do it again. Quiet, now—we've wasted enough time discussing the natural disasters which seem to follow you about. Notebooks out! Jamie, what are marsupials?"

"Marsupials-are-animals-found-in-Australia-and-New-Zealand-which-have-the-characteristic-of-carrying-their-babies-around-in-a-pouch," recited Jamie, while Gemma was scribbling away in the corner of her school planner.

So where are all the mice now?

Don caught most of them and put them into an old trunk, I replied in Wite-Out on the black cover of my Science notebook (easy to disintegrate with a pair of compasses when it's dry—supersleuths never leave traces of secret messages).

How furious were your parents, on a scale of 'earthquakingly much' to 'apocalyptically much'? Toby's green felt-tip tattooed on my forearm.

They weren't at all! I Wite-Outed indignantly. I then ran out of Wite-Out and had to resort to pencil. *It wasn't my fault! It's not as if I'd invited the Pied Piper of Hamelin around for a private recital without thinking of the consequences. Plus, they were too tired to tell me off when they came back. And this morning, too busy hoovering up the little mouse droppings alongside bits of my homework.*

What's going to happen to the mice? Can you keep them? asked Gemma.

Dad's going to release them into the wild far away from college today. You know my parents, they wouldn't be too keen on keeping a trunkful of white mice in the house. They're more into trunkfuls of scratchy blankets.

I don't understand why they'd release them into the wild, though, wrote Toby on my other forearm before I could roll my sleeves

down. *It's not their home.*

If you think my dad is going to ask them all for the addresses of their burrows and take them back there individually, you're painfully deluded, I replied, and buttoned down my blouse sleeves to prevent further access.

No, but I mean, insisted Toby's felt-tip on his own forearm this time, *they weren't in the wild to start with, were they? If they're white mice, it means they're not wild mice. They must be lab mice.*

"Toby Appleyard, what did I just say about kangaroos?" boomed Mr. Halitosis, and we all jumped in the manner of the animal in question.

"Does it have something to do with the pouch?" asked Toby.

"No," said Mr. Halitosis.

"Does it have something to do with the skipping and bouncing and going *boing-boing-boing* across the Australian landscape?"

"No," said Mr. Halitosis.

"Does it have something to do with the

boxing? Apparently if you give them little boxing gloves they start boxing."

"Since when has this lesson turned into a giant game of charades?" moaned Mr. Halitosis. "I was saying, Master Appleyard, that kangaroos . . . Well, what was I saying? Emerald, what was I saying?"

"I'm not too sure, to be honest, Mr. Barnes."

"Ahem—Laura, what was I saying?"

"I can't remember, Mr. Barnes, it was so long ago."

"Well, then," puffed Mr. Halitosis, becoming purpler and purpler, "off you all go! Break time! And I expect you all to come back in having remembered what I was saying!"

Everyone hopped downstairs and into the sun-soaked playground, but the hopping didn't help the remembering.

"Right," said Toby, "what are we investigating this afternoon after school?"

"I can't do anything this afternoon," I groaned. "I have to do that geography homework all over again, because of the attack of the killer

rodents. It's super unfair, I'm not the one who snacks on them, that's Peter Mortimer, and his homework didn't get destroyed."

"Of course it didn't, because he didn't have any, because he doesn't go to school, because he's a *cat*!" said an annoying little voice below me. Looking down, I spotted very near the ground the round face and pair of powerfully protruding ears of one of Gemma's little twin brothers.

"What are you doing here, Fraser?" his sister asked indignantly. "This is the snot-free zone of the playground. Go play with puzzles on the other side with the rest of the toddlers."

"Only if you give me a load of liquid-rich-licorice lollies," replied Fraser before wiping his nose on Gemma's jacket.

"I don't have anything of the sort. Go *away*! Where's Callum?"

"Here," said Callum, who'd been pick-pocketing Gemma all that time, but not very successfully, as he'd found just one lonely Polo mint. "Disgusting!" he declared. "Is that all you've got?"

"Yes," replied Gemma coolly, "this is my school jacket, not Willy Wonka's chocolate factory. Share it with Fraser: you can have the hole, he can have the mint."

Looking irreparably grumpy, the two Oompa-Loompas started walking away, but I hooked them by their collars, struck by one of those genius bouts of inspiration which seem to occur with delightful regularity in my very well-connected brain.

"Hang on, brutish and short little humans," I said. "Do you like jigsaw puzzles?"

"Yes," they chorused.

"Even really really complicated ones?"

"Yes!"

"Even ones where you have to pick the pieces from a pile of mouse droppings?"

"Yes!"

"Do you want to earn yourself a bag of beauteous bonbons? We're talking richer than

licorice, more luscious than marshmallows, and fleecier than cotton candy."

"Yes!!!"

"Good boys. Gemma, call your parents and tell them that we're taking the twins to my place after school for a little game. No need to pick them up until they're done with their job."

Gemma winked and fished out her extremely cool touch-screen 3D-camera phone from her pocket. I patted the twins' probably lice-infested heads, and whispered, "Meet us at three at the school gates. And shush! It's a top-secret mission."

"What on Earth are you doing, Sophie?"

"Just taking the container out of the hoover, yummy mummy of mine."

"Do not call me that. Whatever for?"

"To empty it," I said, which wasn't

technically a lie.

Mum stared at me as if she thought I was going to brew a dark potion with it, and sighed, "The problem with Sophie is that she's a scheming little Iago. What are Gemma's brothers doing in our living room?"

"Right now, not much, but I've found them an activity that will keep them busy. We're baby-sitting them, you see."

"Are you now? You are the least reliable trio of baby sitters I could possibly think of. Where are Gemma's parents?"

"I don't know, doing parent things, probably. Standing in line at the bank, buying a new plant for the conservatory, yawning, that sort of thing."

"Well, you'd better watch that the twins don't destroy everything. You are responsible for them until I'm back, do you hear me, Sophie?"

"Affirmative. Sound reception impeccable. Where are you going?"

"For a walk with your father."

"A walk? Don't you have work to do?" I said, and then gasped in horror because it sounded

so much like something *she* would say.

"Strictly none of your business," snapped Mum (favorite sentence number eleven). And having picked up an oddly-shaped bag, she walked to the car park behind the house, where Dad was waiting for her in the Smurfmobile.

"Why are you driving if you're going out for a walk?" I asked, but she slammed the car door and my words shattered against it into dozens of little alphabet-soup-like letters.

Back in the living room, I emptied the contents of the hoover on to the table in a neat little mountain. Gemma sneezed twenty-four times: her nostrils are stupendously ticklish.

"There you go," I said to Fraser and Callum. "In this hill of mouse poo and dust there are zillions of little bits of paper. Stick them back together on this sheet of paper into the geography homework they used to be, and you'll get enough sweets to turn all the Cambridge dentists into multi-millionaires for the next ten years."

"Let's do it!" yelled the twins, looking like

they'd choose this activity ten times over flying a jumbo jet above a safari park while stuffing their faces with cookie dough ice cream. And within seconds they were as lost in their work as raisins in a bread-and-butter pudding.

"I'm jealous now," I said to Gemma and Toby. "I wish I had a dwarfish sibling to be my minion on a day-to-day basis."

"Just ask your parents for one," suggested Toby.

"No use, they've said many times that after me, they'd never make the same mistake again. Right, let's get ready."

"What's the plan?" asked Gemma.

"The plan is to plant my new video camera on the roof of Gonville & Caius. If the gargoyle burglar comes back, he'll be captured on camera for the rest of the world to see. Just a sec—let me go and get it."

I ran upstairs to my bedroom and, before flinging the door open, stretched my jumper to cover my nose and mouth. The place was infested with Euca-licious: I'd had to spend the

previous night bathed in it. Thankfully, it didn't seem to work, as I was still very un-Gemma-like. I grabbed my swim bag, got the video camera out, and was just about to leave again when I noticed that something wasn't quite right.

I looked around again. The bedroom was the same. But also different. I couldn't figure out why.

"What have you spotted, sleuthing radar?" I asked my brain.

But to no avail. If there was anything that disturbed it, it couldn't tell me what it was.

Shrugging, I went back downstairs, and put on my roller skates in the living-room. Seconds later, I was outside with Toby and Gemma, when suddenly Gemma tripped over something (not the uneven stone outside Chapel for once). As soon as she saw what it was, she rolled to the side, hands over her head as if she expected a hand grenade to explode next to the jasmine bush.

"What's the matter with you?" asked Toby. "Considering a career as a stuntman?"

"I t-t-tripped over Peter Mortimer!" she stammered, standing up again. "I thought he was going to behead me within the next minute."

"Nah, he's become quite the pacifist recently," I said. "Must be all that essential oil I accidentally showered my bedroom in."

But I remembered—a bit uneasily—that his behavior had started to change *before* the oil spill. Toby picked up Peter Mortimer from the ground and pried open one of his yellow eyes with a finger. "He doesn't look too well, Sess," he said.

"He's fine, just a little bit tired from all the mouse hunting," I snapped. "Let's go."

"I think you should take him to a vet. Look, he's like a rag doll."

"You are *so* annoying. When did I ask you to drone on about my cat being one foot in the grave? He's fine. He's just tired. Let's go!"

We left college zigzagging around students, turned into the pedestrian street and sped up to the market place, where we had to do an emergency stop as it was completely clogged

with tourists. Gemma rolled her eyes, Toby sighed loudly, and I was just about to push through a disgustingly slurpy kissing couple when suddenly—a scream!

"Oh my god! Someone get that monster off me! It's going to kill me!"

Everyone spun very fast on the balls of their feet so as not to miss the killing. It was a bit strange at first, since the screamer was dancing around and punching the air like she was battling an invisible creature, until I realized that on her nose was perched none other than . . .

"Herbert!"

Spotlight on Sesame Seade. "Sorry," I said, "he's my hornet. Well, I'm pretty sure. It certainly looks a lot like him. He was accidentally released by my careless teacher. Let me take care of it. Team, give me a box."

Gemma and Toby rummaged around in their pockets, and Toby found a blue pencil sharpener with a big enough container, which he emptied of its little shavings. Like a good hornet hunter, I closed in on the beast, placed the two parts of the container on either side of the screamer's nose, and in a swift and firm movement, locked Herbert into his new cage. Not being of a very accommodating nature, he buzzed angrily for ten seconds, but finally settled down.

"Stationary in the stationery," I said. "Three cheers for Sesame Seade!"

"Hurrah!" everyone chorused, and started clapping, and cried with admiration and happiness, and it was a little bit embarrassing until I realized that people were actually clapping and cheering in the direction of a bearded busker. As if singing *Ob-La-Di, Ob-La-Da* was more heroic than safeguarding the noses of the general public! That's the kind of thing you have to get used to when you're a supersleuth: people are rarely grateful. Grumpily, I grabbed Toby and Gemma and

dragged them away from the bleating guitarist.

"May I remind you we're on a mission? Here, Toby, you're in charge of Herbert. Don't sharpen anything until we find him a larger abode."

He pocketed the insect and we pushed through the crowd like a trio of charging bulls. One minute and sixty-eight seconds later, we were in front of Gonville & Caius again.

"Where are we going to put the camera?" asked Gemma as we crept through the gate, bent double to dodge the laser eyebeams of the Porters.

"Above Jeremy's window. It's in the corner, so it should have a wide enough angle to spot any thief."

"*If* it's a thief," said Toby, "and not the gargoyles flying away of their own accord."

"That is *not* possible," stated Gemma as we emerged into the snowy courtyard, "so there's no need to talk about it." She was so goosebumpy she looked ready to be put into the oven.

We walked up the spiral staircase to the rhythm of her sneezes and

I knocked on Jeremy's door half a dozen times.

"Who's this?" said Jeremy's voice on the other side of the door.

"Your Chief Investigator," I replied.

"Oh. Right. Just a minute."

I counted five minutes until he finally opened the door. But instead of letting us in, he stood in the doorway like a bodyguard.

"What's up?" he asked.

"We've come to install a video camera above your window," I said, producing the pebble-like object. "To catch the gargoyle thief if he comes back."

"What, you want to do that now?

"Good guess."

"Can you come back a bit later?"

"Why? You're here, the room's

here, the window's here, we're here. Just let us in!"

"Have you been wearing lipstick?" asked Gemma, and indeed Jeremy's lips were as rosy as a Disney princess's.

"Why would I be wearing lipstick?" said Jeremy.

"Have you been wearing a pink pashmina?" asked Toby, and indeed behind him on a chair in the bedroom a scarf was hanging that was almost as pink as Jeremy's ears.

"Why would I be wearing a pink pashmina?" said Jeremy.

"Have you been wearing high heels?" I asked, and indeed next to the door was a pair of glittery apple-green stilettos.

"Why would I . . . ?" said Jeremy, but Gemma interrupted him, "I know what it is, Sesame! He's found himself a *girlfriend*! It's either that or he dresses up as a girl in his spare time."

"A girlfriend!" I enthused. "That's furiously smart of you, Jeremy! Does she know about the time you left your rugby kit unwashed for two weeks, and the Porters had to smoke the cockroaches out of your bedroom?"

"I didn't, no," said a voice behind Jeremy. And sure enough, it was, wearing a rather short dress, a pretty blonde girl, whose mouth still had some lipstick left on it.

"Roxanne," sighed Jeremy, "these are Sesame, Gemma and Toby. Okay, come in—install that camera thing, and then go away."

"All right, no need to be so uncouth, we're only doing this for *UniGossip*," I said indignantly. "Don't you want to know who's kidnapped your gargoyle?"

"It's not sky-high on my list of priorities at this very moment," muttered Jeremy.

I skipped inside and got the video camera set up to start recording at eleven-thirty p.m. and cut at five a.m. Toby helped me up on to the windowsill and held my legs while I fiddled with the camera and a roll of

Sellotape to find the best angle.

In the bedroom, Gemma was being polite and making conversation. "So where did you two meet?"

"Oh, just at Clare College," Roxanne replied, "two weeks ago. I'm a student there, and I manage the bar."

"Two weeks ago! It must have been love at first sight, if you're already repainting his face with your lipstick."

"Are you almost done, Sesame?" asked Jeremy in a strained voice.

Gemma prattled on, "Isn't it a bit cold to be wearing a dress like that? Oh, what's that tattoo you've got on your ankle? It's well cool! What made you fall in love with Jeremy? He's all right, I suppose, but there are better-looking ones around Cambridge."

"Have you fallen asleep on that window, Sesame?" groaned Jeremy.

"Nope, it's done!" I said, leaping gracefully on to the floor. "All ready for tonight. Fingers crossed it doesn't rain this time. Right, we

won't bother you any longer, unless you offer us a cup of tea and some biscuits."

"Fat chance," said Jeremy. "Off you trot! And can you *please* text me tomorrow before you drop by to pick up the camera?"

"If I remember. All right, team, let's go! It was lovely to meet you, Roxanne."

"It was, erm, interesting to meet you too," said Roxanne, and we waved bye-bye to her for half a minute until Jeremy pushed us out of his bedroom and shut the door in our faces.

Since trotting is unambitious, we galloped downstairs instead, where Toby threw the door open, but quickly slammed it shut again.

"We can't get out!" he whispered. "Your parents are in the courtyard, Sesame."

"What? My parents? They can't be. They're out for a walk."

I pushed him to the side and looked through the huge keyhole of the old door. Sure enough, it was Professor and Reverend Seade, standing on the lawn and chatting to a gardener. Mum was holding, intriguingly, a box, and Dad

was holding, even more intriguingly, a large butterfly net.

"That's absurd. Since when do they collect butterflies?" I vituperated. "They're always in the wrong place at the wrong time. We need to wait until they leave, now. If they see us, they'll realize we left Fraser and Callum in charge of the house, and I'll get locked in my bedroom with no food until I have to munch on the walls."

"You'd better get used to the taste," announced Gemma who'd been peeping through the keyhole. "They're heading straight towards us."

It's funny how quickly you can move when your life is in immediate danger. In a fraction of a second, Toby, Gemma and I had galloped back upstairs to Jeremy's door. But there was nowhere to hide there—and we heard, one flight of steps down, the door opening, and Mum's fearsome voice filling the staircase, "... because we don't want anyone else to know, you see."

"Higher!" I hissed to Gemma and Toby, and we silently crept up to the second floor. Well, as silently as you can creep up a stone staircase holding a pair of roller skates in one hand. On the second floor, there were three doors. Toby tried the first, I tried the second, and Gemma tried the third. Toby's was locked; mine was locked; Gemma's was not.

"I won the door roulette!" she exclaimed, and we dragged her into the room and closed the door behind us.

"Where are we?" asked Toby as Mum's voice grew louder and louder outside, reverberated by the curvy walls of the spiral staircase.

"Head Gardener's Office," said Gemma. "It was written outside the door on a little slate."

"What? But this must be exactly where they're heading!" I groaned. "Quick—hide in there!"

I opened a large cupboard and we squeezed

inside, alongside a magnificent collection of raincoats. A few seconds later, we heard the office door slide open, and Mum, Dad and the Head Gardener walked in, still chatting away.

"Please, take a seat," said the Head Gardener, and screechy noises indicated that my parents had done so.

"Right," said Mum, "here are some pictures of it. Taken before it escaped, of course."

"I know what they look like," said the Head Gardener. "What makes you think it's here?"

"It must still be somewhere around here. It was last spotted on a roof at Clare College, just down the street."

"And when was that?"

"A few days ago."

"A few days ago? It must be hungry."

There was a silence, and then Mum said, "Yes. It must be *very* hungry. That's why we're worried, you see. Especially as what it eats is so . . . specific."

"I see," mumbled the Head Gardener. "I don't understand why you won't call the police. I'm

not sure I'd be equipped to deal with something like that, even if I found it."

"We can't tell anyone," said Mum. "Even telling the Head Gardener is risky for us. But we need more help. My husband and I, and other people involved in the project, have been looking everywhere for it over the past few days, but in vain. It is *very* precious, you see. We can't let people know about it—if word gets around, someone might try to catch it before we do."

"Then I'll do what I can. Any idea how it escaped?"

There was a pause, and then Dad said, "We suspect it was the claw."

"Oh," murmured the Head Gardener. "*The claw*. Then I'm surprised it's the only one that escaped."

"It's not. More have escaped," said Mum. "But of other kinds. Kinds that blend in more easily, and can go unnoticed."

"Well," said Dad with a sardonic laugh, "*almost* unnoticed."

"Kinds we can afford to lose, anyway. But we need to get this one back."

"I'll do what I can."

"There was another screeching of chairs. "Well, thank you, Mr. Watson," said Dad. "Keep us posted."

"Will do. Have a nice afternoon."

The door opened, closed again, and we all breathed a deep, long sigh of relief. But not for long! For footsteps inside the office indicated that Mr. Watson still hadn't left. And then the tragedy occurred.

ACHAAA!

Time stopped. Heartbeats stopped. The Earth stopped (I think). And then there was light, and the head of the Head Gardener framed in it.

"What is this?" he exclaimed. "Who are you? What are you doing in here?"

"Quiet," I whispered, "or we'll lose the game!"

"What game?"

"Worldwide hide-and-seek. Other kids are looking for us from Timbuktu to Titicaca and

Krakow to Vladivostok. What do you think of our hiding place?"

Judging from the fact that his lips were starting to look like a chicken's backside, I guessed he probably didn't think much of it. Having quite literally lifted us by the collars of our jumpers (Gemma and me in one hand, Toby in the other), he dropped us on to the ground and said, "Did you hear any of that conversation?"

"What conversation?" I asked Toby and Gemma, who, like me, were massaging their throats with pained expressions on their faces.

"Did you hear any conversation?"

"Oh no," said Toby, "I was much too busy being concerned about whether the other kids would find us."

"And I was listening to two moths gossiping next to me," stated Gemma. "One's found a new tasty recipe for wool ragout."

"Listen," hissed Mr. Watson. "You'd better not repeat anything you've heard. Is that very clear? Is it?"

"We won't say anything. We've already forgotten everything about it, and we never heard anything in the first place. But can I just ask a question?"

"Get out of this office."

"Just a cute, tiny, fluffy little question first. That gargoyle that disappeared. Do you know anything about it?"

The Head Gardener went from fuming to flummoxed. "Which one?"

"What do you mean, which one? Is more than one missing?"

"Well, yes," he said. "One disappeared from

First Court two nights ago, and then one from the outside wall of college last night. Why are you asking me this? Do *you* know anything about it?"

"Not at all. Purely out of curiosity."

"I don't like this at all," he grumbled. "I'm calling the Porters!" He dialed a number on his phone and, when it wasn't answered, slammed it down. "You stay here," he growled, "I'll go and fetch them. We're calling your parents, and you'll have to explain yourselves. Worldwide hide-and-seek indeed!"

He left the office, slammed the door, and turned the key in the lock. A second and a half later, we'd opened the window and slid down the nearest pipe to the courtyard. We legged it through the blossom-snowy ground, squeezed like sardines into an alcove while the Head Gardener and the Head Porter angrily strode by, and shot out of Gonville & Caius.

"Phew, that was close," sighed Toby. "I can't believe this, Gemz! Fancy sneezing your lungs out at such a moment!"

"I didn't do it on purpose!" exclaimed Gemma. "Not my fault if I have delicate nasal passages. Plus, it could have been worse—I could have sneezed while Sesame's parents were still in the office."

We wobbled like sherry trifle at the thought. "Well," I said, "at least we learned something from this. Not one but two gargoyles gone AWOL in two nights! I wonder why Jeremy hadn't heard of the second one."

"Jeremy's clearly too loved-up to have noticed anything recently," said Gemma. "You can't count on him at all. People become completely idiotic when they're in love. Like when Toby had a crush on me in reception, and kept making me daisy chains."

"Could you stop bringing that up all the time," grumbled Toby. "It was ages ago, back when I had no taste in girls."

"Right, let's go home and see if the twins have rescued my geography homework. We need to get there before my parents do, or else we're in for some seriously sour scolding."

Energized by the thought, we almost flew back to my house. To my relief, the place still looked like it hadn't been flooded, set on fire, or destroyed by an explosion. We walked in, and Fraser and Callum were sitting exactly where we'd left them, like two obedient dolls.

"How's it going, little puzzle-solvers?" I asked. "All done?"

"Almost," said Callum, sticking a last piece of paper on a sheet. "Here, it's finished!"

"Hurrah! You're my new heroes," I informed them. "I'd kiss you, but I don't want to catch a disease. High five!"

We high-fived, then I popped the cobbled-together sheet into the scanner, and it delivered a new beautiful page of geography homework with barely visible lines where the original had been ripped apart.

"Success! Mr. Barnes can't tell me off. After all, it's all my own work, with a little help from my house elves."

"But it was difficult, Sesame," objected one of the house elves. "You didn't tell us there

were *two* different puzzles."

We all stared at him. "What do you mean, *two* different puzzles?"

We followed the fingers they were both pointing at the same sheet of paper.

A smaller one, a more rugged, yellower, older one, than my geography homework. One that looked like a much-travelled piece of parchment. One from which pieces were missing. And which said, in old, paled, blurry purple ink . . .

One and only one of
the oyles contains the
precious a which, my love
I have enclosed in it. It is in
ur memory, my dear, and
will Rem there forever and eve
Yours tenderly,
Ge

"I know there are some pieces missing," whined Callum, "but it wasn't our fault. We looked for them everywhere. Can we have the sweets now?"

V

Having raided Mum's secret sweet drawer and handed a whole bag of appealing pink pastilles to the twins, the three Sarlands left to be reunited with their parents. Who, instead of going to a funfair or to the cinema, had decided to buy new curtains and a fine-bone china toothbrush holder. Incomprehensible, I'm telling you.

"This mystery is becoming mind-boggling," I told Toby as we walked upstairs to my bedroom. "What was that piece of paper doing in our living room? Who wrote it? And what's an *a*?"

"And what are your parents looking for all around Cambridge?" asked Toby. "Whoa, it *reeks* in here!"

"Sorry, I know," I said, opening the window as he pinched his nose. "It's euca-liciously awful. It wasn't my fault, it's the wind that . . . "

I stopped and stared.

"Have you been turned into stone?" Toby inquired. "You'd make an interesting statue for pigeons to perch on."

"Nothing of the sort. I've just realized something. I know what's changed in here! My alarm clock's facing the wall!" I strode across the room and twisted it back into place. "Oh! And that box of crayons has fallen off my desk. And where's the pick for my electric guitar?"

"There, under the chair," said Toby. "Is it normal to play Spot the Difference in your own bedroom?"

"Someone's been in here," I growled, "and has moved things around."

"Your parents, probably."

"No way. Haven't you seen the note on the door?"

He swung the door open to look at it:

WARNING:
DO NOT TRESPASS
PRIVATE PROPERTY.
ABSOLUTELY NO ACCESS WITHOUT
SPECIAL INVITATION
Trespassers shall be made to walk the
plank OR WORSE
IN THE CASE OF TRESPASSERS BEING PARENTS, THEY SHALL BE MADE TO WALK THE PLANK TWICE OR WORSE.
BURP
YUM
DO NOT EVEN
DREAM
OF ENTERING THIS PLACE
WHEN THE OWNER IS NOT AROUND.
DREAMERS OF THIS SORT SHALL BE FORCED
TO HAVE A BATH WITH STARVING LEECHES
BEST WISHES,
Sesame Seade
OWNER OF THIS BEDROOM AND ALL THINGS
IT CONTAINS*
*APART FROM THE BEDDING, WHICH SHE WOULD LIKE TO POINT OUT IS NOT HERS, BUT IMPOSED ON HER BY TWO CLEARLY COLOR-BLIND PEOPLE WHO CLAIM TO BE HER PARENTS AND DIDN'T LET HER HAVE THE COOL NEON-YELLOW ONE WITH THE GREEN BIRDS.

"Maybe they like the thrill of disobedience," said Toby. "Has anything disappeared from your bedroom?"

"Not that I can see. But things have been *touched*. I do not like my things to be *touched*. If only there was a way to know . . . "

I stopped again, but not long enough to be turned into a statue. "Hang on. There *is* a way!"

I took my fingerprints kit out of my swim bag. Seizing the alarm clock carefully with a corner of bed sheet, I dusted the back of it, detected a couple of fingerprints, and lifted them on tape. Two minutes later, the small microscope had printed them out on to little squares of paper. I compared them to those I already had: mine, and Anthi's.

"One is mine, the other isn't," I announced. "It's not Anthi's either, obviously. Let's see if it belongs to my parents."

Trespassing into my parents' bedroom (they don't have a note on their door, so it's fair game), I lifted the fingerprints off my dad's glasses case and my mum's leftover cup of tea from the

night before. Expectantly, we waited for the machine to print them out, and compared them. But they clearly didn't match the anonymous ones on the alarm clock.

"I don't get it," I marvelled. "Someone other than my parents came to my room and moved my stuff around. But who? And why?"

"Who cares, Sess? They haven't taken anything. You've got to focus on the gargoyle mission."

"Ah yes, that. I've already solved that one, thank you very much."

"What do you mean, you've already solved it?"

"It's as obvious as Halitosis's problem with bad breath. There's something in one of the gargoyles around Cambridge—let's call it the *a*—that their sculptor put in there when they were first built, as some kind of lovey-dovey dribblingly kissy tribute to his loved one. Someone got hold of the letter that he wrote about it, and now that person is going around unscrewing them all randomly from their pedestals to find the *a*."

"That doesn't sound right," said Toby. "There must be some kind of logic to it, or else why would the thief take one in First Court and the other one on the outside wall? Why not take them one after the other?"

"Well, because people would notice if all the gargoyles in the same place went AWOL one by one like deserting soldiers."

"But they *do* notice!"

"Well, yes, but then it would be easier for the Porters to predict which one the thief could target next."

"Perhaps," conceded Toby, but he still looked dubious and I couldn't contest it was a bit of a weak theory. "Urgh, what's that?"

That was the mummified head of a mouse, just next to my bed on the floor, with its little red eyes wide open and a few stringy tendons still attached to the neck. "It's from Peter Mortimer," I said. "He's always bringing me little offerings like I'm his domestic deity. That one must have been there for a while because he hasn't hunted in a few days."

Toby frowned. "It's white."

"Yes, what of it?"

"Well, like I said the other day, there aren't many white mice in the wild. I think this one must be a lab mouse. Like the others."

"Can't be. We aren't at all close to a lab."

Toby grabbed a tissue in his pocket and picked up the head of the mouse. "Do you mind if I take it?"

"Oh please, help yourself to all the corpses you can find. It's not particularly pleasant to tread on them in the morning before you've put on your slippers. Especially when they're still a bit warm. Or worse, swarming with worms."

He pocketed it. "Right, Sess, I have to go. Dad's making a celery and pork scratching purée and I don't want to miss that!"

"You'll be doomed if you don't," I muttered. "I mean, yes, off you go—have a nice evening, Toby! I'll keep you updated on the night-climbing."

"The what?"

"The night-climbing I'm doing tonight, of course. Oh, didn't I mention that I'm escaping

to the roofs of Gonville & Caius as soon as I've tucked the parents into bed? Just trying to identify a thief or two."

"Sounds megafun. But isn't that what your camera is supposed to be doing?"

"Well, my camera is only keeping an eye on the *inside* courtyard in Gonville & Caius. But now that we know that the gargoyle-burglar isn't against some thieving on the *outside* walls, my presence is required."

"Any excuse to stroll around the city at night," said Toby.

"*Supersleuths on skates shall sometimes sacrifice sleep to stalk thieves*," I replied. "Rule number two in the handbook of supersleuthing-on-skates which I'll write one day between two mysteries. Adieu, Toby!"

"Bye-bye!"

But leaving the house he bumped into my parents, who immediately insisted that it was out of the question that he should cycle home on his own at this incredibly late hour.

"It's really not that late," I heard Toby plead

outside the front door. "I do it all the time, my parents are cool with it."

"Well, we aren't," argued Dad. "If you were to disappear on your way home, what would we tell your parents? That we let you go, just like that? Certainly not. I'll drive you home."

"But what about my bike?"

"Sophie can cycle to school with it tomorrow morning and give it back to you then."

And without further ado, Dad dragged Toby into the Smurfmobile.

"Do children often disappear in Cambridge, adorable mummy?" I inquired.

"Well, no, not often, but there's no need to tempt fate."

"When was the last child-disappearance in Cambridge?"

"I don't know, Sophie. Take these plates to the dining room and set the table, will you?"

"Wait, you gave me one too many. There's only three of us, unless Peter Mortimer's allowed a place at the table like I've always said he should be."

"Sorry, I forgot to tell you. We're having a guest tonight. Anthi Georgiades, a visiting scholar from Athens. Lovely woman."

"I know her! Toby almost wiped her off the surface of the Earth. She's also responsible for the terrible smell in my bedroom."

"Oh yes, what's that smell? I've been meaning to ask you. It's infected the whole hallway."

"It's the contents of an entire bottle of *Soothing Luscious Euca-licious Eucalyptus Essential Oil*," I recited. "The wind played coconut shy with it. Apparently Anthi told you she'd bring it to *calm me down*. You're a pair of particularly perfidious parents. Why would you want to calm me down?"

Mum stopped picking cutlery out of the dishwasher and threw me a pensive look. "Eucalyptus Essential Oil. I see," she said, then she shook her head and went on, "Well, clearly, it hasn't worked, since you're your usual uncontrollable self. Get the cheese out of the fridge, please."

"Are you sure it's wise? We don't want another

tsunami of mice. *Tsunamice*. That's a good name for it. By the by, you should know this, as a serial killer of mice for medical purposes: Toby says they must have been lab mice, since they were all white. Is that true, do you think?"

Mum's fingers tightened around the whirring salad spinner. "I don't know," she said coolly. "You're in my way, Sophie—would you please go and set the table?"

"*Oui, maman chérie d'amour*. I'll leave you to focus all your mental powers on the perfect dryness of the salad."

When I tumbled back into the dining-room balancing three wine glasses on four bread plates, I noticed that the side of the sofa had grown a skirt-clad bum attached to a pair of legs in black tights with high-heeled feet resting on the floor. This is a rare occurrence, so I stopped and stared, until the glasses I was holding clinked together and Anthi Georgiades sprang up from behind the sofa like a jack-in-the-box.

"Oh!" she gasped. "Hello, Sesame. I'm so sorry, I didn't hear you coming. I knocked, but

no one came, so I walked in."

"No problem," I said, "we probably didn't hear the knock from the kitchen. Have you lost something?"

"Not at all, no. I mean, yes, maybe. I think I lost an earring here, last time I came to have tea with your parents."

"What did it look like?" I asked, laying the knives and forks around the plates.

"Oh, it doesn't matter. It was cheap."

"No, tell me what it looks like—maybe I've seen it, you see, because we hoovered up the place after the tsunamice, and then I asked toddlerish twins to stick together bits of my homework from the container of the hoover. Maybe my eyes skimmed over an earring in the

pile of mouse poo, and if you tell me what it looks like, *whoosh*! It will all come back to me."

Anthi looked at me blankly, so I explained what the tsunamice had been, and how the puny puzzle-solvers had resurrected my geography homework from the ashes.

She stared at me pensively, and murmured, "I see, that was very nice of them. Well, I guess there's no point worrying about the earring. They would have found it if it was in the pile, wouldn't they?"

"Probably," I admitted. "Would you like an olive?"

She picked a big, black, gleaming one between her long fingers. Her nails were chipped under a glazing of transparent polish. "You sometimes find interesting things in the containers of hoovers. Any funny surprises in that one?"

I looked up at her, she looked down at me, and we had a little game of stern-stares Ping-Pong.

"Nope," I eventually replied, thrusting my

hand in my jacket pocket where the mysterious manuscript was still nesting. "Just my geography homework."

"Shame," said Anthi, smiling. And she popped the olive in her mouth.

☆☆☆

Dinner, predictably (since no one there was my age) was about as enthralling as sorting one's bookshelf alphabetically. Thankfully, I am endowed with dizzying daydreaming abilities, and knitted myself a nice little tale of vengeance, romance, bossy ostriches and flying motorbikes. Between the fruit and the cheese, however, I was rudely interrupted.

"Sophie? Sophie! Are you listening?"

"Wait, let me land safely and turn off the engine." They waited for the maneuver to be over. "Here we go, I'm all yours. What is it, my dear *Papa*?"

He rolled his eyes. "I was just saying, can you please go and get the cracker tin from the cupboard?"

I started the engine again, stood up and wound my way around the table to get the tin out of the cupboard. But when I opened it, it contained just three or four crackers, a whole lot of crumbs, and a dead mouse.

"Would you care for a mouse?" I asked Anthi politely.

"Oh, I'm so sorry," exclaimed Mum. "Those mice! We're still finding them everywhere."

"Including a head in my bedroom," I pointed out. "The rest of the body is probably in Peter Mortimer's belly."

Mum and Dad's heads snapped up to look at me. "He keeps eating them," I said, "It's not a secret. Though he was really useless during the tsunamice. He didn't even lift a paw."

Dad coughed, and Mum said, "I'm sure we don't need to talk about disembodied heads of mice." I thought it was a pity, since it was a much better topic of conversation than historical research, which was what Anthi had been telling my parents about for the past twenty minutes.

When I walked into my bedroom at half past ten, I immediately noticed something new was wrong. The alarm clock hadn't moved, but my pillow had. My electric guitar pick hadn't fallen again on the floor, but a pile of Post-it notes had. My Crayolas were still in their box, but my digital photoframe was laying on its front.

My back grew a little bit chilly from top to bottom, as if a cold wet orange slug was slowly crawling down my spine.

"I'm not scared," I told my fluffy triceratops. His glassy eyes seemed to approve, and so did the other fluffy toys on the top shelf of my cupboard when I opened it to look for midnight-escapade-appropriate black clothes.

I waited for another hour and a half until I was sure from a concerto of parental snores in the next room that they were both right in the middle of their boring dreams.

Before leaving, I reached for my sleuthing kit and got the intruder detector out. It consisted of two electrodes—I stuck one on my bedroom door and the other one next to it on the door

frame, and activated them. Coming back, I'd know if the door had been opened, and, if so, at what time and for how long. As I left my bedroom by the roof, I stuck another two on the outside of the window, concealing them with the frothy jasmine that grows around it.

And then I slid down the big tree, escaped through the little green door, crossed college on tiptoe, and skated away.

VI

Cambridge never completely goes to sleep. Even at midnight, the streets are still swarming with girls who wear skirts the size of belts and boys who bump into streetlamps because they're sporting sunglasses even though the sun's busy warming up the other side of the planet. I swerved around a herd of such people, spotted a Fellow of Christ's College coming straight towards me, hid quickly behind a wall, and he passed by whistling a song that must have been at least as old as Mr. Halitosis.

Taking the busy streets was definitely too dangerous—I turned into a smaller one, but it had a pub in it, from which emerged a whole rugby team. I skated away and rested for a

minute between a small bookstore and a local craft shop, looking up at the crenellated black towers and roofs of Corpus Christi College against the brownish, star-splashed sky. It looked much quieter up there.

Actually, not quite so quiet.

For a dark, slim, nimble silhouette had just appeared on the rooftop.

The burglar!

It had to be. Who else would take a stroll across the roofs of Cambridge in the middle of the night? Especially on a college roof *covered in gargoyles*?

It was time to act. And for action to happen, I needed to get on that roof.

I kicked my roller skates off and hid them in a bush near the entrance to a tiny church behind Corpus Christi. I got my gym shoes out of my pocket (remains of a whole year of learning to walk on beams, which came to an abrupt end when my parents decided I wasn't good enough to become an Olympic gymnast so I'd better focus on the violin, which I then broke).

I put them on and looked hard at the building. I was beginning to find out that I was a real nyctalope, that is to say that I can see in the dark in the manner of the common barn owl. There was a pipe running all the way up the front wall, which could be reached by climbing on the railings surrounding the church, which I did in exactly five seconds.

The pipe was round and far enough from the wall to slip my fingers behind it. I'd had a bit of experience climbing down pipes, which is easy, but climbing up was more difficult. By grabbing it between my knees and pushing

with my feet against the wall, I soon found myself much higher than I would have liked to realize before reaching the top. But the roofs on the other side of the street were like a mountainscape, and I could see the dusty light of the market-place beyond it, and some rare yellow squares with people inside—one working on his computer, another one trying to calm down a crying baby. . . . And suddenly, without noticing it, I was on the very slanted roof

of Corpus Christi College. I high-fived myself, temporarily losing balance, and grabbed on to the closest thing I could find.

Which was a monstrous face.

It took a good minute for my heart to stop hammering at my ribcage like a wacko woodpecker. The monstrous face was just the face of a gargoyle—a monkeyish gargoyle, different from the ones at Gonville & Caius, clutching on to the wall but without a water-spout in its mouth. I tapped its little head and heaved myself onto the nearest window.

The person I'd seen was still there, sitting astride the roof a little bit farther, next to a chimney. It was a young man with glasses, who didn't seem to be doing much else than stargazing. And it seemed like none of the gargoyles on that roof had gone AWOL. Discreetly, I crawled up the roof and started walking on the tiny flat ledge at the very very top of it.

This is when having done a year of walking on a beam becomes a pretty good skill. In fact, I remembered I'd also learned that year to do

cartwheels on a beam. I wondered if I could still do it with the added fun of a drop of death on either side. I tried and managed it absolutely fine. I was going to try another one, until I realized that a pair of bespectacled eyes was gaping at me. There was a long, awkward, heavy silence.

And then the young man said, "That was quite something."

"Thank you," I said, and curtsied. "Beginner's luck, I'm sure. I'd never tried it before."

"You're a kid," he said. "What are you doing up here?"

"Well, what are *you* doing up here?" I asked. "It's not as if it's okay to go on a roof when you stop being a kid."

"I'm a night-climber," he said. "That's what we night-climbers do. We climb up buildings at night and look at the city from there."

"Wow!" I marvelled. "Is that a job?"

"Nah. It's just a hobby."

I sat down next to him. "More interesting than tiddlywinks, I'm sure," I said. "I'm Sesame, by the way."

"Freddy," he said, and offered me a chunk of vanilla fudge, thus becoming my friend forever.

"Thank you," I mumbled, dribbling everywhere like a chow chow chomping on chowder.

"You're welcome. Look at this. Isn't it beautiful?"

It was. The city looked madly medieval from up there, all towers and battlements and pillars half-dunked in random splashes of street lighting. I started composing a celebratory poem in my head, but then remembered I was on a mission, and cunningly asked the night-climber, "Do you like gargoyles?"

"Gargoyles?" he repeated, a bit surprised. "Well, it's not a good idea to grab on to them when you're climbing. They can fall off, and you with them."

"Oh, then I was lucky that one didn't," I said, pointing at my monkey friend.

"That's not a gargoyle," he said, "it's a grotesque."

"A what?"

"A grotesque. They don't spout water, they're

just statues of animals on walls. Gargoyles have a spout running through them."

"So you *are* interested in gargoyles?" I insinuated. "You seem to know a lot about them."

"You have to, when you're a climber," said Freddy. "If you really need to grab on to a gargoyle, you need to make sure it's not too old—because it could just snap—and that it's not too recent, because the recent ones are only loosely fixed."

I gasped. "What do you mean, old ones and recent ones? I thought they'd all been sculpted at the same time! And how loosely fixed?"

"Well, very few gargoyles in Cambridge are as old as the colleges," replied Freddy. "They're fragile, always exposed to the elements. They get covered in lichen and crumble to pieces after a while."

Like the old grumpy one with the Mohawk of moss at Gonville & Caius, I thought.

Freddy went on, "So they have to be repaired or even replaced regularly. Ever noticed how white some of them are, compared to others on

the same roofs? Those are the newer ones. They tend to be more loosely fixed, so they're easier to clean and maintain."

Although I have no evidence for this, I am fairly sure that a light bulb went on in a thought bubble above my head. "Of course!" I exclaimed. "Thank you so much, incredibly knowledgeable night owl. I owe you a whole slab of fudge!"

"You're welcome," said Freddy. "Send it to Freddy Snaith, King's College. Rum raisin's my favorite flavor. Just saying."

"Will do. Okay, I need to climb down this roof and run to Gonville & Caius," I said. "It was lovely to meet you, but I'm on a mission."

"Climb safely," he murmured. "And if you're going to go on the roof there, don't forget you can always escape by jumping to the Senate House."

I shook his hand and slid down to a window lower down, where my grotesque pal was waiting for me. I tapped the tip of his snout, and shuffled down the pipe to the street.

☆☆☆

I decided that skating was too noisy, so I blew a kiss to my faithful wheels under their holy bush and mobilized my sprinting powers. To be honest, running isn't exactly my forte. In fact, if you were to rank the things I can't do (of which there are few), it would probably come in second-highest place, just before "Detangle my hair" and just after "Embroider a handkerchief with my initials." Gran tried to make me do both of these, and failed. Therefore, my handkerchief only says SN, as it's missing the last branch of the M and all the other letters. But I digress.

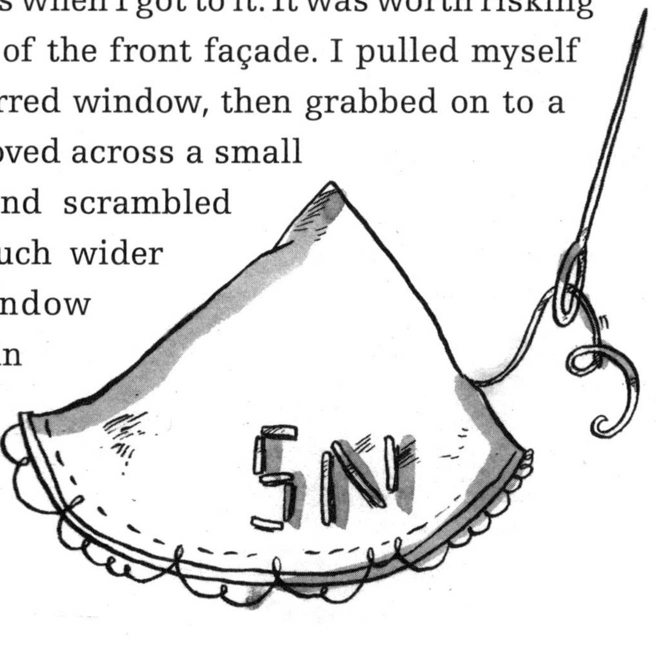

Gonville & Caius was mostly plunged in darkness when I got to it. It was worth risking a climb of the front façade. I pulled myself up a barred window, then grabbed on to a pipe, moved across a small ledge, and scrambled up a much wider bow-window with an intricately sculpted banister. A saint in an alcove was looking very cross as I passed by, but that was probably because he was missing whatever he'd once held in his outstretched hand.

A few more acrobatic moves, and I'd reached the top of the bow-window, which was a small terrace to another window. I threw a cursory glance inside, and only just had the time to flatten myself on to the ledge. It was the office of an important-looking, tea-sipping, book-perusing, bespectacled Fellow.

Thankfully, he didn't notice me.

From where I was, I could see the row of gargoyles on the edge of the roof, and Freddy had been absolutely right—in the dim light of the streetlamp below, some were dark grey and some lighter, and one or two even glowed white. How had I never noticed that before? They were even shaped differently, by the imaginations of different sculptors.

I paused to think. All the little pieces were slowly slotting into place in the manner of

my geography homework, only much more excitingly.

A manuscript had been found which hinted at the presence, in a Cambridge gargoyle, of a precious *a*.

Whatever that was, someone wanted it.

And it had been put there by the sculptor. Therefore, that someone had gone around the place unscrewing the poor gargoyles made by that sculptor to find the *a*.

Had they gotten to it yet? Hard to tell.

One thing was clear, however. That particular someone was Anthi Georgiades.

Anthi Georgiades with her impeccable blow-dries and make-up and high heels, but with the broken fingernails and rough hands of a climber.

Anthi Georgiades who was rummaging around our living room to try to find the bit of manuscript she knew she must have lost there.

Anthi Georgiades whose sphinx-like smile implied that she knew that I'd found it.

And that was a problem.

Especially as Anthi Georgiades was now

right in front of me, black as a panther, kneeling precariously on the slanted roof behind a tiny stone banister, unscrewing a white gargoyle from its pedestal.

☆☆☆

Now, I might be a supersleuth, but I'm only eleven and a half years old and you can't expect someone that age to have had enough time to learn how to do karate on a slanted roof in the manner of a ninja warrior. So I crossed that off the list of possibilities. I also decided I couldn't yell, "Hands up, Georgiades!" as I didn't want the poor woman to freeze with fright and plummet to her death. So I stayed and watched as she carefully chipped at the pedestal, slid the sculpture off it, and stuffed the statue in a backpack. She then put on the backpack and crept up the roof like a spider.

I followed as quietly as I could.

From up there I could see straight into the first court of Gonville & Caius, including Jeremy's dark window. At least I knew I didn't

need to get the camera tomorrow—I'd been there in person to catch the suspect red-handed. Except the suspect in question was running on the roof, not at all within catching distance. I could see she was going to climb down to the lower wall of the college, and I prepared to follow, when suddenly—

"*There!* She's right there!"

Spotlight on Sesame Seade.

And I mean it literally.

A large, shiny, yellow disk of light, directed straight at little me.

Mind you, at any other time, I would have

been thrilled. But at that very moment, standing against a slanted roof and chasing a gargoyle-kidnapper, being trapped in the beam of an eye-gougingly painful torch wasn't exactly as fun as if I'd been in the limelight of a West End show.

And then a voice.

"It's a *child*! I can't believe this! A *child*'s been stealing our gargoyles!"

"Are you expecting me to tap dance?" I asked the unknown person at the other end of the tunnel of light.

I threw a glance over my shoulder. Anthi's dark face was just visible behind a chimney pot. It disappeared in the blink of an eye.

"Don't move,' said the voice. "Put the gargoyle down next to you."

"If I can't move, I can't put the gargoyle anywhere," I replied.

"Stop playing with words and do what you're told until the police arrive!" snapped the person.

"Can't, sorry," I said. "I don't have any gargoyle on me."

My eyes were getting used to the blinding brightness and I could see that it was coming from a nearby window. I made out the shapely belly, white shirt and black tie of a Porter. No risk of him climbing on the roof to catch me.

"Don't lie," he said, "I've just seen you do it. On the outside wall."

"That's where you're as wrong as my parents when they tell me that a spotty skirt doesn't go with a stripy shirt. It absolutely wasn't me. It was someone just as tall as me, but that's because I'm tall for my age and she's clearly short for hers."

"Cut it. Where's the gargoyle?"

"With her. In her backpack. If you want to catch her, you should get a move on, she's escaping that way."

Trying to be helpful, I pointed in the direction of the escapee, but the torch light didn't even flutter that way.

"Stop lying!" shouted the voice at the end of the light. "Answer my question: *where is the gargoyle*?"

Rolling my eyes, I turned around, which is not uncomplicated when you're leaning against a steep roof. "Look," I said, "I haven't got anything. My pocket isn't even big enough for anything more than . . . "—I looked inside—"a small pen-sized flaslight, a shopping list (scrunched up), and a hairband."

Little rectangles of light were starting to hatch all around the first court of Gonville & Caius, as people woken up by the spectacular scene were looking out to see what it was all about. It was a tricky situation, as one of them might recognize me.

And one did.

Jeremy Hopkins, at his window, was mouthing things to me, which I had no idea how I was supposed to understand, but which clearly meant he Had a Plan.

And the plan came in the form of a huge *BANG!*

Two seconds. That was all I needed. Two seconds for the Porter to swing the beam of light to the other side of the roof, and then

swing it back again. But when it swung back, it shone onto an empty slice of roof, as I wasn't there anymore.

I was two, three, four chimneys away, hugging a turret, and below me the sirens of an oncoming police car were bawling their way through the streets of Cambridge.

That's when Freddy's words printed themselves neatly before my eyes in a brilliantly helpful connection of my stellar brain.

Don't forget you can always escape by jumping to the Senate House.

The Senate House, situated just in front of Gonville & Caius, is a huge white Greek-looking building where people go to collect their degrees wearing hilarious hats and giggle-inducing gowns. The two buildings are far enough apart on the road, but I'd never noticed how close their roofs were.

I could jump it. I could. I had jumped much longer distances. I wished I had my wings again—for I had wings once, as you should know if you've read the first volume of my adventures.

And if not, why not? Do you generally start a book series right in the middle? You are an odd sort of person.

I looked at the gap and the drop underneath it. I thought of my legs pedaling through the air if I missed. I thought of my parents' sad faces at my funeral, whimpering, "Alas! Woe! She wasn't such a bad daughter after all. When I think of all the times we sent her to her bedroom with no dessert! When I think of all the times we forced her to do the dishes!" On my tombstone would figure the following epitaph: *Sesame Seade, sensational supersleuth. Sufficiently scolded, seldom scared.*

So, to live up to that epitaph, I launched myself into the skies.

And landed quite easily on the flat roof of the Senate House.

"Pfsha!" I scoffed. "That was disappointing."

I quickly found a way down to the street via a few pipes and compliant stones, and landed agilely next to the police car. Light beams were crossing all over the place and policemen were

shouting orders, making the front of Gonville & Caius look like a fairly bad *son-et-lumière* show, but I knew they wouldn't catch their thief tonight.

I looked at my watch. Half past one in the morning. Definitely time for bed.

So I skipped merrily away to where my roller-skates were hidden, and went home.

VII

RING RING! RING RING!

"Yes, right, alarm clock, I've heard you!"

RING RING! RING RING!

"Shut up now! Why won't you shut up? Why?"

Because I'd been tapping my bedside lamp instead of the alarm clock, as my eyes informed me when I opened them. When the world stopped being blurry, I spotted the ringing alarm clock, which was, inexplicably, on my *desk*.

I jumped out of bed to turn it off. Had I moved it to the desk before going to bed when I'd crawled back in? I didn't have any memories of that. And one of my drawers had been opened. And my school uniform was in a pile on the floor.

I swallowed what felt like a mouthful of

thistles. Someone had been in my room again, whether while I was away or even—*gulp!*—as I'd slept.

But at least I could know *when* they'd been in.

I checked the electrodes on the window. They informed me that the window had been opened and closed again at one thirty-seven in the morning. But that was when *I* had sneaked back home. So the intruder must have come in through the door.

Except that the electrodes on the door stated that it hadn't been opened all night.

I turned around slowly to face the bedroom. And cleared my throat.

"All right," I said, trying not to quiver. "I know you're still in here, whoever you are. I know you came in before I . . . before I left yesterday, and . . . you haven't left. I'm going to find you."

Where the intruder could be hiding was a bit of a riddle, to be honest. My parents, in their immense generosity, made sure my bedroom was the smallest room in the house. Even the spare bedroom is bigger than mine. They argue

that double beds need bigger rooms, but I don't know how they can know that without speaking fluent Furniture. From what I could tell, there were only two places where a person could have been hiding. Under the bed, and in the closet.

Wielding a lime-green highlighter, which was the sharpest thing I could find, I knelt down next to my bed. Slowly, tremblingly (but not as tremblingly as most people in my situation), I lifted the duvet to look under the bed.

Nothing.

(Well, apart from half a dozen discarded pairs of pants and socks, some colorful candy wrappers, a few pens, a squash ball, a broken remote-control for a car and a small Eiffel Tower Liam had brought me back from his last trip to Paris.)

I breathed deeply, stood up again, and reached towards the handle of the cupboard door. It slid open smoothly as I pulled it. I brandished my highlighter.

Nothing.

(Well, apart from piles of not-particularly-

well-folded clothes, scattered shoes, ugly coats, and my shelf of games, toys and fluffy toys.)

"I don't get this," I muttered to the tremendously trespassed-upon bedroom. "I don't get it."

Knock knock knock, went the door, and Dad's exasperated shout, "Sophie! Are you awake? You're going to be late for school if you don't take your shower soon!"

"Coming!"

Absent-mindedly, I gathered my clothes and school stuff, reactivated the electrodes and walked downstairs, trying to iron out the perplexed look on my face. I didn't want to worry my parents with tales of invisible intruders undetected by modern technologies who might very well still be lurking somewhere in my bedroom.

When I came back from the shower to munch on a bit of toast, Mum lifted her head from her newspaper, which she normally doesn't do just for me, so I assumed she had a question. She did. "Where's Chubby?"

Chubby is the ninny nickname my parents have endowed Peter Mortimer with. I've told them hundreds of times that it isn't right, but they persist in calling him that, just like they won't drop the inexplicable Sophie to refer to me.

"Peter Mortimer, you mean? I don't know, he must be around. He's been a bit tired these days. He didn't even notice I was sitting on his tail the other day. You'd notice if someone was sitting on your tail, Mum, wouldn't you?"

Mum and Dad exchanged dark glances, and Dad said, "Yes, darling, we'd realized he was a bit unwell. We think we should take him to a vet this morning. Is that okay with you?"

"Sure," I said, dumping three spoonfuls of raspberry jam on my piece of toast. "Make him super-aggressive again. I'm fed up with having a cat that's such a wet blanket."

"I'm sure the vet will do her best," said Mum very calmly. "Can you find him, and put him in his little basket?"

"I can, though I don't approve. What would *you* say if I put you in a little basket?"

"We've discussed this before, Sophie, cats do not go in cars without being in a basket. Just do it, please."

So I swallowed the rest of my breakfast, brushed my teeth, and ran upstairs and downstairs and into the kitchen and into the bathroom and opened a few windows and finally found Peter Mortimer roasting in the sun on a windowsill, still as limp as a lump of pizza dough. He didn't even mind when I put

him inside his wicker basket and closed the lid. This is the moment when my arms usually get joyfully shredded and the multitudinous seas incarnadine. Nought of the sort then, and the cat didn't even meow with indignation.

I brought the basket to Mum, who was getting ready to leave.

"Thank you, Sophie. I'll take him to the vet this morning."

And suddenly and incomprehensibly, she dropped to her knees and put her hands on my shoulders. "What's this display of affection, Mother?" I asked. "I'm not sure I'm prepared psychologically for a cuddle."

She sighed, "The problem with Sophie is that she's a cold-hearted little Miss Havisham. Listen, darling. I'm sure the vet will do her best, but Chubby does look *very* unwell."

I slammed my palms against my ears. "La-la-la, I'm not listening." But my palms aren't completely sound-proof, so I could still hear her droning on.

"Ignoring problems won't make them go

away. I'm just telling you that I think it could be wise to prepare for unpleasant news."

"*Non* and *niet* and *nein* and even *no*," I declared. "Make it pleasant. I want Peter Mortimer back here tonight in perfect health. I demand it. Anyway, bye-bye everyone, I'm going to school."

And I struggled out of her arms, batting my eyelids like a loony because my eyes were prickling for no good reason, and went to pick up my roller-skates.

"Wait, Sophie," said Mum, standing up again. "Don't forget you have to cycle to school with Toby's bike."

The whole world was being very contrary today. I huffed, puffed, crammed my roller-skates into a bag, tripped over that stupid uneven stone outside Chapel like a mere adult—it resonated weirdly throughout First Court—and finally left the college on Toby's flashy bike. Mum, meanwhile, was backing the Smurfmobile down the driveway with Peter Mortimer in the basket on the seat next to her. I pedaled furiously away,

swirling around clusters of slow-walking people. Unpleasant news indeed! As if I had any time to waste thinking about that.

I focused on the problem at hand. Anthi Georgiades was the gargoyle thief—that was for sure. But how could I denounce her? She knew that the Porter of Gonville & Caius had seen *me*, and not her. She'd be quick to ask the Porter to confirm that *I* was the one on the roof. And she'd probably gotten rid of the gargoyles already, and would simply say that I was lying. The camera I'd planted on Jeremy's window wouldn't be of any help—we were in a completely different part of the college, and she would have had no reason to go near enough to appear clearly on the film.

It was the trickiest situation since the day a Fellow found me at two o'clock in the morning gorging on Eton mess in the college kitchens. In fact, it was even trickier than that, since the Fellow was also coming for seconds, so we parted good friends with many meringue-flavored hiccups.

In a word, it was tricky.

Just as I was wondering what to do, my phone buzzed in my pocket. I alighted on the pavement, precariously perched on Toby's ridiculously high saddle (he isn't even taller than me, so it's just for show). It was a text from Jeremy:

Glad you managed to escape, you foolish funambulist. The bang was from one of the

firecrackers you gave me, by the way. Good foresight. Any news?

I was getting late for school, so I typed manically:

Thanks. Would have been disemboweled by parents without you. Yes, I know who the thief is. But sticky situation. Will drop by this afternoon and tell you.

As I waited for my ludicrously lazy phone to send my text, I glanced at the cars stopped at the red light, and lo and behold, there was the Smurfmobile with my mother inside, on her way to work at the Pharmacology labs. I raised a hand to wave at her and wish her to make a lot of money today by discovering a vaccination against ingrowing toenails, but my sleuthing radar picked up a suspicious frequency.

"Why is she not still at the vet's?" I asked a fire hydrant next to me. The fire hydrant didn't know.

Inside the car, on the passenger seat, was

the little wicker basket, presumably still with Peter Mortimer inside.

"Strange," I went on to my mute red friend. "The vet is entirely in the opposite direction. Do you think Mum's taking Morty to the vet *after* work? I hope not, he'll get bored if she leaves him in her office for a whole day."

My sleuthing radar was now on full blare, and there was something else there, a nagging feeling of something not-quite-clear in Mum and Dad's expressions that morning when they were telling me about Peter Mortimer.

The light went green, the Smurfmobile's engine started, and I followed from a distance. As we passed by the school, I spotted Toby in his usual place, waiting for Gemma and me to arrive, but I hid behind a bus and cycled straight past. There are things that are more important than school. Like cats.

Ten minutes later Mum turned left into the road that leads to the Pharmacology department, and parked outside the main gate. I tied Toby's bike to a road sign and slowly walked up to

the white building in the shadow of the trees, watching Mum take out Peter Mortimer's basket from the passenger seat. From her panting as she carried it to the front door I knew he was still inside it—he's not exactly the slender young cat he used to be.

Mum stopped to rummage around in her bag, found her university card, swiped it, the door opened, and she walked in. I don't know why she makes everything so complicated, when a ground floor window was wide open.

Two minutes later I was hiding behind the last row of seats in a small lecture hall, with Mum at the front.

Soon a handful of people in suits walked in, shook hands with Mum as enthusiastically as if she were going to show them an action movie and hand out popcorn, and sat down in the front row. Mum closed the door and cleared her throat. The big screen behind her had two words on it: *PROJECT ATARAXIA*.

"Dear colleagues," said Mum, "I am delighted to see you all today, three years after Project

Ataraxia began. I am also delighted to be able to tell you that the money was well spent, as we are very close to devising a range of Ataraxia pills for both human and animal consumption."

This seemed to please the colleagues to no end, as one even cheered, thankfully covering the noise of my phone buzzing again. I got it out—it was a text from Toby:

> What are you girls doing??? Are you together??? Halitosis is like WHERE ARE GEMMA AND SOPHIE and I'm getting all the nuclear fumes.

Keeping one side of my brain focused on Mum's presentation—she was going through extremely incomprehensible drawings of funny-named molecules—I texted back:

> I'm not with Gemz. I'm on a mission. I'll be there asap. Tell Halitosis I've twisted my ankle and am therefore walking very slowly to school.

"In short," Mum was saying on the stage, "the formula has been found, and lab mice

have reacted well to it, though the effects do not last for very long on them—three to four days, at most. However, in larger mammals, the effects have been found to last for two to three weeks, which is a very good sign. They work, furthermore, not only on lab animals and domestic animals but on wild animals, which is what we always wanted to achieve."

Someone in the audience whistled, and interrupted Mum: "This sounds very interesting. Wild animals? Such as?"

"Well," said Mum, "you will all remember cocoa from your visit to the lab last year."

The audience mumbled that they did, and I thought it must have been pretty good cocoa if they all remembered it a year on. But Mum's next sentence made it clear that it was, in fact, Cocoa with a capital C rather than cocoa, the hot chocolate drink.

"Cocoa was given to us by a zoo, as they could not put up with her anymore—she had undergone some serious trauma and as a result, as you no doubt recall, she was *very* wild.

Unusually for her species, she kept attacking her peers and biting the carers. Well, she reacted extremely well to the treatment; two days later, she was as docile as a fluffy toy. We had been treating her for five months, and she showed no signs of bad temperament all the while."

"*Had* been?" asked someone in the audience. "Where is she now?"

Mum's face flushed quite visibly, and she coughed. "Unfortunately, this is where the bad news starts. We have reason to believe that the claw kidnapped her, as well as a very large quantity of lab mice, and *released* all of them."

There was a shocked silence, punctuated by another buzz of my mobile phone. Cursing, I extracted it from my pocket, checking that no one else had heard it—but everyone in the lecture theatre was too busy being bamboozled. Another text from Toby:

> Well, dunno where Gemz is, then. She isn't there nor her little bros. Get here quick!

I typed back, *Will do my best!*, just as a woman in the audience broke the silence.

"That's terrible. Even the claw should know better. Surely Cocoa cannot survive in the wild."

"She can't," said Mum. "She's been missing for a week and a half, now, and we fear the worst. It is a huge waste, and we've been doing everything we can to find her, but to no avail. As for the mice, they unexpectedly reappeared just a few days ago, in my living room. The medicine had lost its effect on them, though."

"So Cocoa is lost," said the woman in the audience. "And with it, all we know about the reactions of big mammals to the medicine, am I right?"

"Well," said Mum with a triumphant smile, "not quite."

And she crossed the stage to Peter Mortimer's basket.

"It is a very happy coincidence," she said, "that my daughter's cat apparently happened to eat one or more of the mice who still contained some of the medicine. And the effect is working

on him, from what he's eaten."

"He wasn't wild to start with, though," objected the woman.

"Not technically," smiled Mum, "but trust me, he was not an easy-going cat. I could never have done this before he accidentally swallowed some Ataraxia."

She opened the basket, and lifted Peter Mortimer by the skin of his neck like a vulgar rabbit!

"Of course," she said, "as a result, Chubby here has become extremely valuable. We did not know that the substance could be transmitted in that way, and it is obviously a phenomenon we have to study. He will therefore stay here in the lab for as long as is necessary, while we collect information about him. Meanwhile, we will start experimenting on primates and ultimately humans."

"Primates and humans?" asked someone. "So, for now, we don't know how they react to that drug?"

"We still need to test it," said Mum, "but it

should be a fairly quick process now. And we're also working on a pill, rather than an injection, to make it easier to give to people. Especially to children. At the minute, we've got it to look like this."

The screen behind her switched to another picture.

I recognized what it was.

And I gasped so loudly this time that there was no way that anyone in the room could have missed it.

But I didn't care that all of them were staring at me as if I'd just materialized out of thin air. I didn't care that Mum was flabbergastedly uttering a very great number of *Sophie Margaret Catriona Seade*s. All I could think of, as I stared and stared at the picture, was—

THAT is the bag of pink sweets from Mum's secret drawer that I gave to Gemma, Fraser and Callum yesterday.

VIII

"This has to be," stammered Mum, "this *has to be* the most outrageous, the most scandalous, the most shocking, the most . . . the most . . . indescribable thing you've ever done in eleven and a half years of existence!"

That broke me out of my reverie.

"You're one to talk!" I shouted, and turned to the audience. "She kidnapped my cat! She told me she was taking him to the vet! She was going to keep him here in this dire lab for who knows how long!"

I dodged Mum's arms and ran downstairs to pick up Peter Mortimer, who was looking contentedly at everyone else. "You are the worst mother ever!" I yelled at her. "Next time I meet

Cinderella and Snow White for a kebab, I can tell you we'll bond over our respective tales!"

"I am so terribly sorry," said Mum, but not to me, to the audience. "Sophie should be at school, and I am going to take her there right now. Sophie, leave that cat here."

"No."

"Put that cat down immediately."

"I refuse."

"Sophie, I am very serious."

"Me too."

She grasped Peter Mortimer's lower body, I held on to the top half, and I thought for a minute that we were going to end up with half a cat each. But one of the women in the audience stood up and walked towards me.

"Here, Sophie," she said in a soft voice. "I'll

be the neutral party in this. I don't think it's right of your mum to have taken your cat, so I'll take him with me, okay? I promise I'll keep him safe until we decide what to do with him."

Mum glared at her in a way which would make the strongest sumo wrestler burst into terrified sobs, but the woman just glared back, which instantly won my trust. "Okay," I said. "You'll be nice to him? He likes tuna."

"I'll give him tuna," she said.

Mum reluctantly let go of Peter Mortimer and I handed him over to the woman, who put him back into his little basket and got ready to leave.

"The claw isn't wrong, you know, Agnes," she muttered to Mum as she passed by.

"Typical of you to be so angelic, Helen," replied Mum in a voice that made icicles grow on all the walls.

"What's the claw?" I asked, but no one replied.

"You are coming with me," hissed Mum, "and you are not to say a word."

"I have something important to . . . "

"Not a *word*, Sophie. *Not. A. Word.*"

I wondered if I could find a way of communicating the message "Gemma and her little brothers have accidentally swallowed a whole bag of your wacky pills" without saying a word. I got a notebook out in the car, and wrote it down, but my hand was shaking and the car was whirring and Mum snapped, "What are you doing, thrusting this in front of my face? Do you want to have an accident?"

I shook my head like I was trying to make a cocktail inside it, and lifted the notebook up again, but she said, "Stop it." And it was the most stoppingly "Stop it" I'd ever heard, so I stopped it. But I got my phone out, typed the same message, and sent it to her. Her phone vibrated in her pocket. She looked at me, looked at my phone, and said very calmly, "Did you just send me a text, Sophie?"

I nodded. She parked the car alongside the pavement, breathed deeply, took her mobile phone out of her pocket . . .

. . . and threw it outside the window on to the

road, where it shattered into dozens of pieces which got run over by a lorry.

She then turned to me and asked, "Is that clear?"

I nodded. She started the car again, and two minutes later she stopped in front of the school.

When I left the car my legs were trembling so much I thought I was going to cause an earthquake.

☆☆☆

"That was *exactly* what I meant to tell you," said Toby to me at break. "I thought there was something dodgy about Peter Mortimer, and I wondered if it could have come from his food. That was why I wanted to keep the head of the mouse, to analyze it for traces of weird substances. But I'm not good enough," he concluded, shaking his head. "It's really advanced biology."

"Don't worry, Toby—it's great that you've still got the head. It means we've got proof that this substance was used, even if my mother and her pals try to destroy the rest of the evidence."

"True," he said, looking happier.

I certainly wasn't as happy. I hadn't told Toby about Gemma and the twins yet—partly because I didn't know if that was why they weren't at school today, and partly because I knew it was my fault for giving them the sweets. I'd told Toby everything else—the midnight escapade yesterday, the gargoyle thief whom I couldn't denounce to the police, the creepy invisible intruder in my bedroom, and my mother's presentation.

"What's that pill for, then?" asked Toby.

"Making wild animals less wild, apparently," I replied. "If you want to put them in zoos or something, I guess."

"But why would they check if it works on humans?"

That hadn't struck me until now. "I don't know . . . I guess, maybe some humans . . . would need to be calmed down?" But as I said it I realized how chilling that sounded. And I remembered Mum's voice—"*Especially children*."

"Oh, I think I know," I murmured. "They want

to give it to kids who are too active. To *calm them down*, like Anthi's Euca-licious essential oil, except *that one* would work."

"Blimey," whispered Toby. "When that drug comes out, Sess, I bet you'll be the first on the list of victims."

He was tragically right. I pictured a future where I would be a pale, plaited, plain, placid little teenager offering custard creams to guests and spending hours learning the harp.

"Will you still be my friend when I've become a huge bore?" I asked Toby.

"Don't think so," he replied. "But don't worry about me, I'll find someone else to hang out with. Hey, where's my bike?"

"Uh-oh, it must still be parked outside the Pharmacology Department. And if I go there again I'll get hanged, drawn and quartered by Mum. And I can't call her to tell her to bring it, because she's assassinated her own phone. Maybe you could go after school, if I lend you my roller skates? We can meet up in town afterwards, I'll be there anyway to buy fudge for Freddy—the

one who told me about the gargoyles and the escape through the Senate House."

"I'm sure I won't fit into your roller skates," he said. "I'm a boy, I have big feet."

We compared foot size, and he was exactly the same as me, which he was incredibly

disappointed about. I handed my precious purple roller skates over to him. And then both our phones buzzed, and it was a text from Gemma:

> Sorry not at school today. Me and the twins are feeling really tired. Hope you're well. Keep me updated on the mission.

"So the whole Sarland siblinghood is out of order," I said in as calm a voice as I could manage. "Wonder why."

"I'll write her a text to update her on the situation," said Toby.

And he wrote:

> You're missing out on all the action!!! Sess chased her mum with PM in car to Pharma lab coz PM ate a mouse with drug in it! The drug is for making children calm! So S's mum's crazy furious coz S was found out and then she took her to school so now I don't have my bike! And the claw was mentioned again—WHAT is it?! Also yesterday night S went

roof-climbing and met 1 cool guy with fudge, but then spotted Anthi—lady I almost killed—stealing a gargoyle BUT then SHE (S, not A) was spotlighted by Porter and escaped when JH exploded a firecracker! So S can't denounce A! Also S's bedroom's got an invisible intruder in it! Not under bed or in closet! Anyway get better soon xx

I said, "I'm not sure Gemz will understand everything, but good effort." And indeed, half a minute later, Gemma sent another text saying:

The Prime Minister ate a mouse???

Toby sighed, "And to think that that text cost me the price of five."

"That's enough! Toby and Sophie, you haven't been listening to anything I've said so far during this lesson. Toby, take your stuff and move to the other side of the classroom, next to Emma. *Now.*"

Toby rolled his eyes and gathered his

notebooks and pencil case. It was absolutely untrue that we hadn't been listening to what Mr. Halitosis had been saying—one half of my brain was entirely focused on the marsupials of Australia. But the other half was concentrating on exchanging little pieces of paper with Toby about the seriously sticky situation I was in. And now I was deprived of his company, so all I could do was listen to the lesson. As if marsupials were going to save the Sarlands' lives, frame Anthi Georgiades, and make my parents love me again! (If they ever had.)

"Right," said Mr. Halitosis, "Emerald, I asked you to prepare a presentation on kangaroos, koalas and platypuses for today. Have you done it?"

"Yes, Mr. Barnes."

"Come to the front, then, and tell us what you found."

Emerald walked up to Mr. Halitosis's desk with a few pieces of paper and began to read out her notes. "Kangaroos, koalas and platypuses are exclusively found in the wild in Australia.

The kangaroo is a very common animal there. . . ."

Meanwhile, I tried to *think*. How could I prove that Anthi Georgiades was the gargoyle-thief? The only solution was to sneak into her room in college and take pictures. But maybe she'd already destroyed all the evidence, since she knew I was on the case. Of course, I still had the manuscript, but I couldn't show that it was linked to her. If anything, *she* could then argue that *I* had found it and was stealing the gargoyles to find the *a* for myself.

". . . The koala only eats one sort of plant: the eucalyptus plant. It's got a pouch for its baby, sleeps most of the time, and it is wrong to call it a koala bear, even though it does look a little bit like a teddy bear. . . . "

As for the Sarlands, I wondered if I could tell Dad about it. He could be as scary as Mum, of course, but at least his religion placed *Thou Shalt Not Kill* as number one on the top ten of big no-nos. And we had to do something—the drugs had never been tested on humans, after all, and they must have eaten a whole lot of pills.

". . . An interesting thing about the koala is that its fingerprints are very much like human fingerprints—in fact it's easy to mistake one for the other. . . ."

But what was Mum thinking about, leaving a bag of dangerously appealing pink pills in her secret drawer of sweets and chocolate? Parents could be so careless. Surely it wasn't my fault if . . . suddenly I realized that Toby, on the other side of the classroom, was staring at me intently, with eyes so wide open that I could have slipped a couple of saucers in them, though I didn't try, for want of saucers.

"*What?*" I mouthed.

He pointed at Emerald and did his insistent look again. First I thought he was telling me off for not listening. But then I looked at what she was holding up, and understood.

"And this is what the paw print of a koala looks like. Now, let's go on to talking about the platypus. The platypus is a strange animal with the bill of a duck and . . ."

My brain, which, I daresay, employs an

extremely good sort of butler, rewound for me the past five minutes of Emerald's presentation, and extracted all the important info:

1) *koalas eat eucalyptus leaves.*
2) *they look like teddy bears.*
3) *their fingerprints can be mistaken for human fingerprints.*
4) *their paw prints are exactly like those I'd found in the flower bed at Gonville & Caius, and in First Court at Christ's.*

To this, my brain-butler added, "If I may, Madam—just a suggestion—do you think perhaps this might be the species of animal that 'Cocoa' belongs to?"

So I turned to Toby, and I mouthed to him, "*There is a koala in my bedroom.*"

And he put both thumbs up, and mouthed, "*Wicked!*"

IX

Anyone who says kids these days don't do anything is as wrong as Toby's conjugation of the verb "to have" in our last French test. As soon as school was over, I jogged to town, while Toby skated away to get his bike. I had a to-do list which wouldn't have fitted on a whole roll of loo paper.

First stop, the Fudge Kitchen. I'm a girl of my word.

"Can I have a slab of rum raisin fudge, please?"

"No. It has alcohol in it. You're too young."

"It's not for me, it's for someone who's old enough."

"I've heard that before."

"Give me a coffee and nut slab, then."

"Are you allowed coffee?"

Adults can be so obtusely obfuscating. I took a deep breath. "What do you have that's appropriate for very young children like me, then? Baby formula fudge?"

"Chocolate and pistachio?"

"Deal."

I grabbed the bag, crossed the street to King's College, and popped the appropriate fudge in Freddy Snaith's pigeonhole. I left the college again and sprinted down the street until I quite literally bumped into Jeremy. This was okay for me, as his chest isn't exactly muscular, but it was less pleasant for him: my

skull, being in charge of protecting my super-brain, is particularly hard.

"Sssesssam-eigh!" he coughed and spluttered. "What are you doing here?"

"Running home. I need to unearth a koala from my closet, and then find some eucalyptus leaves to feed her with, or else she'll die. If she isn't already dead. Where do you buy eucalyptus leaves from? I've never seen any in Sainsbury's."

"Your life is complicated," he sighed, which I couldn't deny. He rummaged around in his pocket. "I was just coming to see you. I thought you'd need *this*." And produced the pebble-sized camera.

"No need, the thief won't be on the film," I said. "And anyway, I know who's done it."

"Do you? Wonderful!"

"Not as wonderful as you'd think. I have no evidence." And I quickly told him about my disastrous self-incriminating investigation.

"Okay," he said, "so you're in a bit of an ever-so-slightly problematic little situation."

"Yes. Jeremy, you have to publish an article

in *UniGossip*, it will give more weight to my denunciation of Anthi."

"Sorry, Sess, I can't do that and you know it. You'd be my only source. It's not how journalism works. Until you find enough evidence on that woman, I have to keep quiet on the matter."

My phone buzzed, saying *Toby*.

Hey, Sess. Where are you?

Not far, I typed.

Not far from what?

From a boy on a red bike wasting phone credit.

He looked around and saw that he was standing right next to me.

"Curses! I'll have to ask my parents to top up my phone *again* after today. And for nothing. Where are we going now?"

"To my bedroom to find Cocoa," I said. "And then we'll go explore Anthi's room."

"Cocoa? Why cocoa?" asked Jeremy.

"I'll explain later. See you around, Jeremy! Hope everything's going well with your girlfriend."

Judging by how red his cheeks became and the silly smile he produced, I assumed things were going fine.

Three minutes later Toby and I arrived at my place, rushed through the front door and ran upstairs. I threw my bedroom door open and stopped.

"Okay," I whispered. "Let's not frighten her."

"She must be half-dead with hunger," remarked Toby, "so even your face shouldn't cause too much of a reaction."

Slowly, I opened the closet, and browsed the top shelf.

A fluffy triceratops. A teddy with a Christmas hat. Two cats. A piglet. An owl. A snake. A gruffalo.

And a koala. Asleep.

"What do I do?" I mouthed to Toby. "I've never held a koala before!"

Toby crossed the bedroom, stood on tiptoe, and gently lifted the koala to cradle her into his arms. "Hello, Cocoa," he whispered. "How are you? Bit peckish? You thought you'd find

eucalyptus here because of the smell, didn't you? Tough luck."

Cocoa opened an eye like a shiny little obsidian marble and closed it again, not too bothered.

"What do we do?" I asked. "We need to find eucalyptus leaves for her. Where are there eucalyptus leaves in Cambridge?"

Toby thought hard for a minute, then—"Got it! At the Botanic Garden, of course. They've got all the plants in the universe there."

"Toby, you're a genius! Let's go. But what

should we do with her? We can't leave her here, what if my mum finds her?"

"Let's take her with us to the Botanic Garden," said Toby. "It's the only way to keep her safe. If we need to leave her there, I'll ask the Head Gardener to look after her—I know him well, he's pals with my mum."

It sounded like a bit of a gamble, but that was the only plan we had, therefore it was automatically the best one. "Okay," I said, "let's put her in a backpack and get there at the speed of light."

"Wait," said Toby. "What's she got in her pouch?"

He shuffled her around a bit. Her little black hands were reaching for the pouch on her belly. "Oh no," I murmured. "Don't tell me she's gone and sprouted a *baby*."

"Impossible," said Toby, "they'd surely control that in the labs. No, it's something else. Must be something she collected somewhere . . . "

And before our staggered eyes, we watched Cocoa take out of her pouch a small, round package, wrapped in old-looking paper and loosely tied-up with string.

Some of the paper had been torn, and underneath, just showing through, was the glittery, shiny, prismatic, rainbowy facet of something that looked incredibly *precious*.

"It's the *a*," I marveled. "It's the *a*! Toby, Cocoa found the *a*!"

"What? How? Wasn't it supposed to be in a gargoyle?"

"It must have been, but listen to this—it must have been in the very first one that was stolen! Maybe it fell out and the thief didn't notice. But Cocoa was in Gonville & Caius that night—we know that, because we saw her paw prints in the grass and in the flowerbed. She must have found it and taken it with her! And then, the next night, she came to Christ's and

settled into my room. The thief—or rather, the thieves—have been stealing more gargoyles thinking that the *a* was in another one, when it was in my room all that time!"

"Excellent, thank you. Now please give it to me, and we'll part good friends."

We gasped, and turned around. Anthi Georgiades was standing in the doorway.

"What are you doing here?" I asked.

"The door was open, and I felt like getting my piece of manuscript back. But this is *so* much more interesting. Give me the precious object."

"The precious object! You don't even know what it is," I snarled. "That piece of the manuscript has always been missing, hasn't it?"

"It doesn't matter. I know it's precious, and I want it."

"I know you do," I said, "and I won't give it to you."

Anthi sighed, walked in and sat down on my bed. "I mean it's precious *to me*, not just because it's expensive. All right," she said. "I'm going to tell you a little story. You like stories, don't you?

You're kids. Listen to this. It's a nice story."

"No time, sorry," I said. "We've got a koala to feed."

But she'd already started. "Once upon a time, there was a sweet British gentleman called George Carter. He was a sculptor. He made the loveliest statues. He did mostly restoration work, though—that's what paid the most, in the 1950s, after World War II, when buildings had to be repaired. He chiseled beautiful neo-Gothic columns, carved scary gargoyles and grotesques, made all the old buildings look new again."

"Sounds like a great guy," I said, "but Cocoa needs to binge on eucalyptus leaves right now."

I could as well have been talking to the TV. Anthi went on, "One day, George went to Greece on a special grant to study sculpture. It was his first trip outside Britain! He was very excited. There, he met a gorgeous, clever young woman named Eugeneia. They fell in love, got engaged, got married, had a baby girl. The delivery didn't go well, however, and Eugeneia died.

George was heartbroken. He could not stay in Greece—too many painful memories. So he took the baby back to Britain, and continued his work there as a sculptor. The University of Cambridge hired him to repair some of the gargoyles and carve new ones. Gonville & Caius in particular asked him for several new gargoyles. A few years later, he died. He had never remarried and had no family left. The little girl, Clara, was therefore sent back to her mother's family, in Greece, where she grew up, fell in love, married, and had several children of her own."

She paused and smiled. Toby said, "Including you."

"Including me, indeed. Unfortunately, just a few months ago, the family was hit by big financial problems and had to move out of the old house for a smaller one. It was time to sort through all the papers that had been accumulating in the attic for many, many years—some of which had belonged to Clara's mother and father. My grandparents."

"And that's where you found the manuscript," I guessed.

"Yes. It was in a very bad state. Maybe some mice had already had a go at it. But I understood the most important thing about it. That my grandfather, in memory of my grandmother, had hidden a precious object in one of the gargoyles he'd carved for Cambridge. How precious exactly, I couldn't know, but I knew he must have earned a lot of money over the years, as he was so famous in the trade. All I knew was that I needed to come here and find it. So I came, and I located all of his gargoyles, and stole most of them and broke them up into little pieces, but couldn't find the *a*. Until now. I'm incredibly grateful to you, Sesame. And you, Toby. But now, you've got to give it to me, because you see, it's really mine."

There was a pause, during which we all watched Cocoa pat her protuberant pouch pensively.

And then I said, "No, it's not yours. It's not yours at all."

"What do you mean?" retorted Anthi, looking slightly annoyed now. "I've just told you the story; it's mine."

"No. You think the story says it's your grandfather's. In fact, it says it's Cambridge's, really. He wanted it to stay here."

"He's dead, so it's my heritage. Give it to me."

"He never intended for you to have it. He just wrote a note to himself in a moment of despair and you found it. It doesn't give you any rights over it at all."

"You're just children, you don't *understand,*" snapped Anthi, and she got up and walked towards us. I stood in front of Toby and Cocoa with my arms widespread like a mother goose protecting her eggs.

"You are an idiot, Anthi," snapped Toby behind me. "I can't believe this. Can't you see what you've done? You've broken every single one of your grandfather's gargoyles. You've broken what was *really* precious about him—his work! What he'd devoted his whole life to!

And all that for what? Just for that little object? You're really stupid."

Anthi winced. Apparently, that was something she'd never thought about. "Stop it," she muttered. "Please. Give me the *a*. Please."

"Nope," I said.

"I have a black belt," said Anthi.

"And I have a shiny turquoise one," I said, "but I can't see how it's relevant to this."

"In judo, I mean," she said. "One move, and both of you will be on the floor."

"I think not," I replied. "I have good reflexes."

"Supercool," said Toby, "there's going to be a fight."

"There absolutely is *not* going to be a fight," said the last voice in the world I wanted to hear at this very moment. "This is my house, my daughter, and my koala. Get out of here immediately or I'll call the police."

Having stated this, Mum turned to Toby and said, "Now, I will take Cocoa, if you don't mind."

I whispered to Toby, "Front window."

Then I said to Mum, "As a matter of fact, we do mind."

And we disappeared.

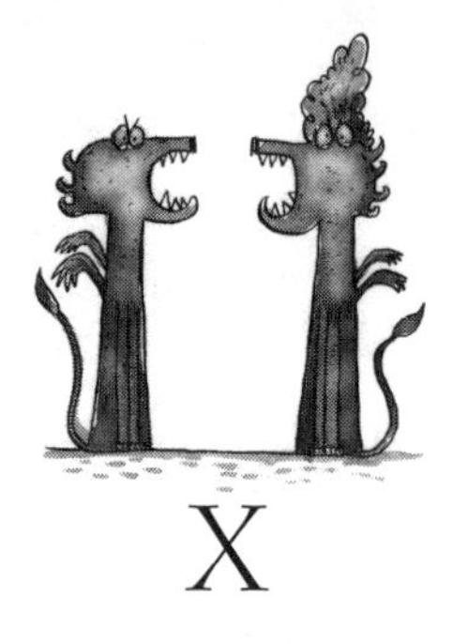

X

A second later, we'd climbed down the wisteria and landed in First Court.

"What now?" shouted Toby. The two adults were tumbling down the staircase inside the house. We had five seconds. We could run away into the street through the front gate. We could rush to Second Court. We could hide in Chapel. Or we could . . . *What was that?*

That was the jingling sound of my brain saving the day again. While one side of it was frantically trying to think of a normal, boring escape, the other side had noticed the slab of stone that was slightly irregular outside of Chapel. The uneven stone that Dad, Don and I had tripped on. And which, my brain

remembered, had made a strange empty sound when I'd half-fallen on it.

"There!" I yelled, and caught Toby by the collar. I kicked the slab of stone aside—it revealed a black, gaping hole.

We leapt into the void.

And landed, thankfully, not too far down, on rubbly, damp, sloping ground. A white triangle cast from the opening was the only source of light. A few meters above our heads, on

the surface, Mum and Anthi were trying out many different ways of asking "Where have they gone?"

"Sesame," said Toby. "What *is* this place?"

"I don't know," I murmured. "I've lived here all my life, and I had no idea about this underground thing. Is Cocoa okay?"

"I think so. She doesn't seem like the kind to ask if we're there yet."

I fished my tiny pen-sized flashlight from inside my pocket and switched it on. It shot a thick beam of milky light into what looked like a long underground passage, mostly cluttered with earth and rubble, but where stone foundations were still visible.

"It must be super old," I said. "And probably man-made, unless we're about to meet a particularly gigantic mole."

"Are you sure we need to walk down?" moaned Toby. "What if it's a crypt with skeletons? What if we stay stuck down here forever? I think I'd run out of subjects of conversation after a while. And then we'd have to eat Cocoa, not even cooked."

"We can always walk back. Come on, Toby, be a bit adventurous! We've always wanted to find a secret passage."

And a spooky secret passage it was. With stalactites of rock spindling down from the arched ceiling, and crumbled-down bits of stone in places, and drops of muddy water plopping down onto our heads. We walked for what felt like an eternity, but must have been about five minutes, and then we spotted a square of yellow light close to the ground.

"Where are we now?" stammered Toby, who'd spent so much time trembling I was worried he might have given Cocoa brain damage.

I knelt down to look through the square. "Wait a minute," I said, "I recognize that place . . . It's . . . it's . . . "

I crawled through the opening, which was right underneath a wooden bench, and stood up in the middle of—

"Clare College Cellars!"

"What?" huffed Toby, who was just squeezing

through the square as well, but has a bigger bum than me. "What's that place?"

"The cellars of Clare College," I said. "They're an old crypt that has been turned into a student bar. Remember? I investigated them two weeks ago or so. *Strange noises* had been heard here. But Jeremy decided to close the case, because there wasn't enough evidence. . . . "

I twirled around, and my eyes met those of someone I'd last seen wearing not much pink lipstick.

"But of course," I murmured. "He closed the case, because *Roxanne* told him to. Didn't you, Roxanne?"

"I did indeed," said Roxanne offhandedly. She got up from the chair she was sitting on. "Sweet boy, Jeremy. When you're in love, you'll believe anything. I convinced him easily that there was nothing to investigate. As the bar manager of Clare Cellars, I knew better than him that there hadn't been any strange noises at all."

She was wearing a short skirt, and I could see her ankle. The ankle Gemma had spotted a

tattoo on. The tattoo of an animal paw, baring its claws.

"*You* are the claw?" I asked.

"Well, not just me. I'm the president."

"The president? So it's . . . what, a secret society?"

"Of course. It stands for the Cambridge League for Animal Welfare," replied Roxanne calmly. "We're animal activists. We like animals, so we protect them. Stealing them from labs and releasing them into their rightful environments is something we often do, for instance."

"I see. And you think a city is the right environment for a koala?"

She raised her eyebrows. "How do you know about the koala? And to begin with, where have you come from?" She looked at the floor, and bent down to look under the bench. "Oh. I see. Gosh, I'd never spotted that hole before. It probably used to be covered with a ventilation

grid. *That* must be how they escaped."

"Escaped? Who escaped?"

"Well, the mice and the koala, of course. We'd locked them inside the Cellars until we could release them properly into the wild. We'd planned to ship the koala to Australia. But she escaped before we could. Where does that thing lead to?"

"To Christ's College," I replied.

"Interesting. Must be an old disused passage. You haven't found the koala, have you?"

We shook our heads firmly, but unfortunately, that was the moment Cocoa chose to start climbing out of the backpack. She opened her huge black eyes, and Roxanne did exactly the same.

"The koala!" she exclaimed. "Fantastic, she's back! Give her to me, I'll take care of her."

Toby shook his head. "No. We don't trust any of you people. All thieves and liars. We're taking her to the Botanic Garden."

"Don't be ridiculous," snapped Roxanne.

"We are *not—being—ridiculous*!" shouted

Toby. He swung Cocoa into his arms, and grabbed my hand. "Come on, Sess! Let's get away from here."

We whooshed upstairs into the explosively sunny first court of Clare College, followed by Roxanne who was running terrifyingly fast. "Quick! That way!" I yelled, and clutched Toby by the arm to swerve towards King's College. We barged through a group of tourists who screamed abuse at us in a language we didn't understand and ran alongside the huge Chapel. I checked over my shoulder—Roxanne had got stuck in the group of tourists. We buried ourselves in the busy streets and sprinted down to the market place, where I had to stop, panting.

"What do we do?" asked Toby.

"First . . . I . . . try . . . to . . . get my breath . . . back!"

"You are so useless at running, Sesame! And your lungs don't function properly."

"Maybe . . . but . . . I'm a genius . . . at everything else." I caught my breath. "Okay . . . Let's try and

see if we can sneak back . . . into Christ's. To get your bike and my roller skates. The Botanic Garden is far away—we need wheels."

"What if your mum and Anthi are still there?"

"They won't be, they must be looking for us everywhere in town, so they won't think we've gone back there. Let's go."

We tiptoed into Christ's through the back door, and Toby unlocked his bike while I squeezed into my roller skates. "Here," I said, "give me Cocoa." He handed her over to me, and we left the place again . . .

But not before running into the malefic duo we were precisely trying to avoid. One of them (Mum) was on a bike. The other (Anthi) was on a shiny red Vespa. "Here they are!" screamed Anthi.

"Leave them alone!" shouted Mum. "Do not approach them! That's my daughter! Sophie, come here immediately!"

"Pedal like your life depends on it!" I boomed to Toby, and we whizzed down the street into the busy road.

Cocoa, I think, had fallen asleep in my arms. Nothing you can do will impress a koala. Even skating at a thousand miles per hour on a hectic road, honked by all the cars and tailed by three nutty grown-ups.

We turned into a smaller road, and then down a much bigger one, and suddenly, on my right, Anthi materialized on her Vespa in a flash of red and black.

"I'm faster than you," she said. "Give me the *a*."

"No!"

We swerved apart to avoid a taxi, but she closed up on me again. "Give it to me!"

"Sesame!" yelled Toby. "Here!"

And he *lifted his arms above his head*.

"Are you sure, Toby?" I screamed. "Hands-free riding?"

"I know I can do it!" he shouted.

Anthi's left arm shot out, but it was too late. I'd already thrown Cocoa into the air with a strength I'd never had in any cricket match.

Cocoa was still asleep in mid-air, and just blinked and yawned when Toby intercepted her

with both hands.

I'm telling you, nothing you can do will impress a koala.

Toby cycled straight into the Botanic Garden, and I followed on my skates. The lady at the till jumped out of her booth, squealing, "What is this?" and, not being able to catch us, decided to focus on Anthi and Mum instead. "You are not coming in with your bikes and motorbikes!" I heard her exclaim as we tumbled down a green pathway, and another one, and another one, past a row of greenhouses, past the big central lake, and all the way to the depths of the Botanic Garden.

"The eucalyptus plants are there," whispered Toby, finally jumping off his bike.

"I'm so proud of you," I said. "Cycling without your hands and without killing anyone or even yourself!"

"I've always known I could do it," Toby exalted. "Look at Cocoa! She's so happy."

"Happy" wasn't exactly the right word for it. "Gluttonously wolfing down an inordinate quantity of eucalyptus leaves without bothering to breathe" would be closer to the truth. It was nice to watch, though. I like seeing people enjoying their food. Except when I see Toby enjoying his father's food, which is the darkest mystery I've ever encountered and one I shall never solve.

Above our heads, the birds were chirping, and we could see shreds of blue sky through the leaves of the trees. It looked like a perfectly quiet, restful, lovely afternoon in the forests of Australia.

Except Roxanne was there.

"Good idea," she said. "Bringing her here to feed her. You kids are full of good ideas."

I rolled my eyes. "What do you want, Roxanne?"

"The koala. For her own good."

"We don't trust you," replied Toby. "In fact,

we don't trust any of you. Go away!"

I wondered who he meant by "any of you," and following his stare I had the displeasure to encounter those of my mother and Anthi. But also an older, mild-looking man, as tanned and shrivelled of face as a sundried tomato.

"Oh, Mr. Lorenzo," sighed Toby. "It's good to see you. Can you tell these people to go away, please?"

"I've tried," stammered the old man, "but they won't listen. What is this about?"

Anthi took a few steps forwards. "Okay, we've finished playing games now," she said (why do adults always think we're playing games?). "Give me the object now! I can see it. Give it to me. It's in your hand."

"I won't give it!" said Toby, and hid his hand behind his back. "And, er, anyway, that's not it."

"Do you think I'm an idiot?" asked Anthi. "I can see it. Give it to me!"

And she pounced.

On her tree, Cocoa didn't look even slightly concerned for the boy who'd given her a free bike

tour of Cambridge. Such churlishness! I made a move to help Toby, who was valiantly battling black-belted Anthi, but he shouted, "No, Sess—don't—get back to the tree—you can't let your mum—or Roxanne—get to Cocoa!"

So I leapt back quickly enough to serve as a human shield to Cocoa. Her pouch, strangely enough, was still bulging. Leaning forward discreetly, I pulled it to look inside.

Inside was the *a*, still wrapped up in paper and string.

But then—what was it that Toby was trying to protect?

"I've got it!" screamed Anthi.

And she stood up triumphantly, holding a little round object wrapped in tissue. She was holding Toby down by the neck, which he looked strangely okay about. In fact, he was even whistling.

"I've got it," Anthi chanted, "I've got it! I've got the *a*!"

"You don't even know what it is," snarled Toby.

"No," she said, "but I soon will!"

With an expression of delight on her face, she tore the bit of tissue apart. And I saw what it was, and made a very, very big effort not to burst out laughing on the spot.

"It's in a box," she announced. "In a little plastic box. How interesting."

"You have no right to take that!" declared Mum.

"What cheek," I said, "when *you* took my cat!"

"Shush," said Anthi, "I'm trying to open it."

She comically failed to do it with just one hand, which entertained us all for a few seconds. Grumbling, she finally stuck half of it in her mouth, and pulled hard on the other side.

And bingo! The box opened.

"Earthquake mode!" I yelled to Toby, and I grabbed Cocoa and plunged to the floor.

I'm glad we'd had practice with that, as it turned out Herbert the hornet was *not* happy about the facilities the pencil sharpener had

offered him in the past day or so. And apparently, he had decided to let everyone know he had complaints.

So strategically and decidedly, he settled on the following stinging order:

1) *Anthi (on the nose)*
2) *Roxanne (on the cheek)*
3) *Mum (on the arm)*

before whizzing furiously out into the fresh blue skies, freer than ever.

XI

So the police arrived (the lady at the till had had the good idea to call them), and I was delighted to see my old friend the Inspector emerge from a leafy alley in the manner of Dr. Livingstone.

"Sesame Seade! What are you doing here?"

"Hullo, Inspector! Good to see you again! Just supersleuthing, as usual. Here's another bouquet of criminals for you."

"Goodness me, what did you do to them?"

"I didn't do anything. They had the misfortune of aggravating a stripy friend of mine."

"I would suggest rushing them to hospital," said Toby. "I'm not sure how much bigger Anthi's nose can get before it explodes and covers us

all in pus, blood and snot."

Indeed Anthi was now the spitting image of a proboscis monkey.

"Can we get a ride in your car?" I asked the Inspector sixty-eight times, and ultimately he groaned, "Oh, go on, then."

And he put the siren on, and in the manner of Moses parting the Red Sea, all the cars, bikes, taxis, buses and pedestrians in Cambridge split to the sides of the streets before our very eyes to let us pass.

Roxanne was charged with stealing animals, Anthi was charged with stealing and destroying gargoyles, and Mum, somehow, wasn't charged, because apparently she hadn't done anything wrong. As for Cocoa, she stayed in a zoo near Cambridge for two months, gobbling down gazillions of eucalyptus leaves, and was ultimately shipped back to a reserve in Australia. She never sent as much as a postcard. Koalas are greatly ungrateful.

The enigmatic thing is that the *a* got lost. Probably in the fight, or before, or after. Who knows? The policemen who searched everyone didn't find it at all.

But then it's true that, when they searched my jacket pockets, they didn't seem to notice the hole in one of them. A hole that was due to a hoglet having stayed there for an afternoon. A hole just big enough for an *a* to slip into it and settle comfortably into the lining.

Where would you put an *a*, if you had one?

That was the question I asked Toby and Gemma at school a few days later. Gemma and

the twins were back to normal health, thanks to an antidote discreetly given to Mr. and Mrs. Sarland by my extremely apologetic mother. Funnily enough, she forgot to mention she was the cause of their children's mysterious illness.

"You could sneak back into Gonville & Caius and stick it into another gargoyle," suggested Toby.

"It might fall off in the rain," said Gemma.

"It still needs to go back to Gonville & Caius," insisted Toby. "That's where George Carter intended it to be."

"Hang on," I said. "I know exactly the right place for it."

We coated the little package in clay to make it look like a round stone, and the next evening I sneaked out of Christ's and climbed up the front wall of Gonville & Caius again. But this time I stopped next to the grumpy saint in his alcove, who'd lost whatever he'd been holding in his hand.

"Here's a replacement," I said. "You'd better look after it properly this time."

The next morning, I dragged myself downstairs for breakfast like a prisoner about to be executed. The Seade family life has never been the most kissy-cuddly-tickly in the history of parent-child relationships. But the past few days had been particularly nippy. In fact, every word the parents had uttered in my direction since that afternoon at the Botanic Garden had triggered mini-blizzards in the living room. It had reached the point when Dad's "good night" the night before had sounded like the most adorable thing anyone had ever said to me.

And this morning, apparently, was not going to get any warmer, judging by the blood-red copy of *UniGossip* on the breakfast table, blaring in bold black:

STUDENT GARGOYLES GONE AWOL? LOST TREASURE AT GONVILLE & CAIUS

DRUGGED KOALAS AND "TSUNAMICE": VOICELESS VICTIMS OF MEDICAL RESEARCH

"Your friend Mr. Hopkins," said Mum behind me, "has managed to make it sound like I'm a crazy boffin trying to turn everyone into sleepwalkers, and slaughtering animals for the pleasure of watching them die."

"That sounds about right," I muttered.

"Meanwhile," she said, ignoring my comment, "there's someone here who'd like to be reunited with you."

She went to the kitchen and came back with a wicker basket that was hissing, spitting, roaring, meowing, growling and bawling.

"I don't know why you love that cat so much," she groaned. "It's the nastiest pet in the world."

I swallowed many times because my throat felt tight, probably because of hay fever. "Thanks for bringing him back," I said. "But I still haven't forgiven you for abducting him in the first place."

"Well," she declared, "I still haven't forgiven you for ruining my presentation, raiding my sweet cupboard, letting me get stung by a hornet, and passing on all that slanderous information to your journalist friend."

"Okay," I said. '"I think we're even. Maybe we could swap forgivenesses."

She said, "I think that's a fair deal."

I presented my hand to shake on it, but instead she decided to squeeze me against her chest as if it was something normally done in the Seade bower. I tend to forget that she's all warm and soft and smells of jasmine, like a tea-scented duvet, so I focused on storing that memory for about a minute or two.

But the basket was starting to get destroyed from the inside, as Peter Mortimer's claws ripped at it like it was woven with spaghetti.

"Right, we need to open this," sighed Mum, letting go of me. "He doesn't sound too *chillaxed.*"

I gaped at her and she smiled at me, and I tried not to laugh, but you know when you try not to laugh and you end up distorting your face like you've just gulped down a whole ladleful of chili powder?

"Ready?" asked Mum.

"Ready!" I said.

She breathed in and out deeply. "Right. Opening in 5 . . . "

"4 . . . "

"3 . . . "

". . . 2 . . . "

". . . 1 . . . "

. . .

OUCH!!!

Acknowledgments

Sesame might not have known it at the time, but my reading of *The Night-Climbers of Cambridge* (reprinted in 2007 by Oleander Press), by the pseudonymous Whipplesnaith, allowed me to ensure that all her night-climbing, including the big jump from Gonville & Caius to the Senate House, would be absolutely safe and completely unperilous—not that any readers should try it!

Thank you so much to Rachel, who enthusiastically took on the editing of the series from Ellen. Big thanks too to Kirsty, to Rebecca, and to my friend-and-now-editor-Lauren! And last but not least, to Sarah, for giving life to Sesame through her amazing drawings.

Don't miss Sesame's first adventure,
***Sleuth on Skates*!**